Skulduggery

A RINEHART SUSPENSE NOVEL

A RINEHART SUSPENSE NOVEL

SKULDUGGERY

A YELLOWTHREAD STREET MYSTERY

WILLIAM MARSHALL

HOLT, RINEHART AND WINSTON
New York

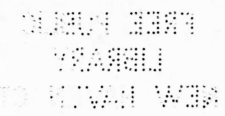

First published in the United States in 1980 by Holt, Rinehart and
Winston, 383 Madison Avenue, New York, New York 10017.

Library of Congress Cataloging in Publication Data
Marshall, William Leonard, 1944–
Skulduggery.
(A Rinehart suspense novel)
I. Title.
PZ4.M372Sk 1980   [PR9619.3.M275]   823   79-1933
ISBN 0-03-047491-4

First Holt Edition: 1980
Printed in the United States of America
1 3 5 7 9 10 8 6 4 2

The Hong Bay district of Hong Kong is fictitious, as are the people who, for one reason or another, inhabit it.

Trompe L'Oeil

There was a thick white midwinter morning mist coming in from the South China Sea. Whisper and phantom-filled, it rolled in billows from the still, bitterly cold ocean, slid into the typhoon shelter on the point of Hong Bay, and then moved up and across the seawall into Hong Kong itself. Coming down, it lay in the streets and lanes and alleys and then moved slowly up the sides of buildings, closing over their storied windows one by one while people slept. It was 5.30 a.m., eyeless dark and silent in the city: the mist moved in and caped it.

In the artificial harbour of the typhoon shelter, a yellow light blinked. It was a marking buoy—the mist thickened and obscured it and set the brass bell tolling on its framework. The sea was very still: the mist moved the buoy back and forth in a steady knell. Then the bell stopped and there was only the sound of the lapping of the sea against the seawall and, here and there where the sandy bottom was higher, the sound of the water on sand and pebbles. The mist thickened. It covered the island of Hong Kong and turned lights and neon illuminations into candleglows. The mist in the streets picked up smoke and vapours in its pores and turned grey. It slid across the face of the island like a tattered unwashed sheet. It was cold and death-clammy.

Far out to sea where the mist had come from, there was the deep-gorged blast of a foghorn from a big ship. The mist condensed against welded steel plates on the hull and turned them icy. Rivulets of moisture ran down painted railings and

I

ladders. There was the sound from the sea of hatch doors being slammed closed and locked as the crew of the mist ship hurried below down passageways to find somewhere where there was warmth and the smell of cooking. Then there was another foghorn a long way off and the answer call of the first ship as its pilot hunched over a radar screen in the darkness on the bridge and watched for blips. The buoy's bell began tolling again, and then the two foghorns called to each other simultaneously and then called again.

In the streets near the seawall, a few people too thinly clothed for the cold rubbed their hands together and moved a little more quickly on their way home. Along Beach Road, a lone taxi switched on its fog lights. Inside, the driver turned up his heater. The heat blew swiftly into the cab and made it a haven. The taxidriver peered along the sidewalks for fares. The sidewalks under the yellow argon fog lights were dim blurs: he thought anything might come out of that mist—a shape would signal him and he would stop to pick it up, something—something misshapen, up from the sea . . . he switched off his FOR HIRE sign and turned for home.

Through the mist, a craft came slowly into the typhoon shelter. It carried no foghorn nor crew and the water pushed gently across its surface, sluicing it down. It was a wooden raft six feet square, made buoyant by oil drums at each corner. It carried no sail nor rudder and the objects laid out on it were all dead. It bobbed into the typhoon shelter and paused there, caught briefly in gentle turning currents. A piece of rope attached to one of the objects trailed gently back into the water: it left a wake where it moved in the undulations of the sea. Nothing on the raft moved or was nonplussed by the lack of forward motion—the raft had no destination. A hundred and twenty yards from the shore, it turned slowly and silently on its axis. Something rolled towards the stern where the rope was and then rolled back again as the current ebbed and was gone.

The raft, a blur in the moving mist, went infinitely slowly towards the shore. On it was a long white object (the mist

2

seemed to move through its outline) and other smaller things laid out on the blackened wood deck alongside it. A deviant wave came from nowhere and lifted the raft an inch or two against the downward pressure of one of the oildrums—and there was a clicking noise like two dice being touched together —then the wave was gone back to the sea and whatever it was that had touched returned to its original position and was still.

On Beach Road, a police car prowled cautiously down towards Great Shanghai Road. It passed by the stone wall marking the limits of the New Hong Bay Cemetery, accelerating slightly as the Chinese driver calculated the height of the wall and how easy it would be for something to come over it. There was a faint light at the edge of the cemetery. The driver thought it was the lantern outside the newly installed cemetery-keeper's hut. It looked faint and distant. A bell somewhere out in the harbour began tolling again and then stopped.

The police driver locked his door surreptitiously and hoped his partner would not see. His partner touched his revolver holster. The police car reached the precinct edge of Hong Bay and swung up into Yellowthread Street to go back to the Station. The driver leant forward and turned up the two-way radio. It was silent. No one was on the streets. He thought that at the Station the radio operator was probably having a steaming cup of tea and telling someone a funny story. He turned up the heating in the car and tried not to think about cemeteries.

The raft halted in the centre of the typhoon shelter and bobbed up and down, its cargo still and uncaring. A sampan slid past a hundred yards away, but the boatwoman, swathed in headscarves, saw nothing. She worked unhurriedly at her stern oar, washing the currents with its blade. There were faint shafts of light starting through the mist as sunrise came, but they were wan and grey and too high up to illuminate the flat raft on the water.

The sampan and its boatwoman passed back into the mist.

The raft caught the dregs of the oar's wash and turned towards the seawall and the beach. It caught a current going into shore and moved laboriously with it, grounded against the edge of a sand slope on the beach with one corner and turned full length against it, then began to slide back to sea again. A second wavelet turned it back.

The edge of the raft caught against a rock on the beach and lodged. A third wavelet pushed it against the rock and held it. Something on the raft rolled down the length of the deck towards the sea, but it struck another object at the stern, moved it, and was caught against the line of the trailing rope.

The bell out in the mist-enshrouded sea began tolling for the objects on the raft to return, but they were landstuck and did not return. They stayed on the beach, a complete and fleshless man's skeleton with its ankles roped together, a dead fish, a mound of some sort of vegetables, and three other smaller objects, until sunrise, when they were found by the sampan woman returning from her fare.

The vegetables were sweet potatoes, ten of them. They were fresh. The skeleton, unclothed, picked clean, its bones in places turning to dust, dead for at least fifteen years, had obviously only purchased them for eating the day before.

Even in the obscurity of mist you could tell that the skeleton had intended to eat the potatoes—it had its complete set of false teeth, upper and lower, laid out neatly on the raft next to them, and, for good measure, a spare, longer tooth that came to a Vampire fang point lodged firmly in one of its empty white eye sockets.

The other object on the raft, caught up in the trailing ankle rope, was a dead Priacanthus niphonius, and, attached to the trailing end of the rope, unrusted from immersion in the water, was another object.

It was, of all possible things, a ten-inch length of three-and-a-half-inch diameter galvanised iron drainpipe—painted blue.

The bell stopped tolling and there was no sound anywhere.

4

Hong Kong is an island of some 30 square miles under British administration in the South China Sea facing Kowloon and the New Territories areas of continental China. Kowloon and the New Territories are also British administered, surrounded by the Communist Chinese province of Kwantung. The climate is generally sub-tropical, with hot, humid summers, cold winters, and heavy rainfall. The population of Hong Kong and the surrounding areas at any one time, including tourists and visitors, is in excess of four millions. The New Territories are leased from the Chinese. The lease is due to expire in 1997, but the British nevertheless maintain a military presence along the border, although should the Communists, who supply almost all the Colony's drinking water, ever desire to terminate the lease early, they need only turn off the taps. Hong Bay is on the southern side of the island and the tourist brochures advise you not to go there after dark.

1

The hour of 8.45 in the morning found Detective Inspector
Phillip John Auden riding up and down in the elevator in the
Cathay Gardens bachelor apartments in Hanford Road. Detective Inspector Phillip John Auden would have been found
riding up and down in the elevator in the Cathay Gardens
bachelor apartments on Hanford Road any time that morning
since 6.15 a.m., and, to Detective Inspector Auden's vertigo-
polluted mind, it looked like a very strong possibility that the
said Auden would be still found riding up and down in the
said elevator until Doomsday.

Auden said to the elevator, 'Bloody elevators!' and leaned
back into the corner of the two person aerial room and got the
sleeve of his coat dirty. He thought, "Bloody *elevators!*"

*Licensed to carry two adult persons or one adult and two
children, or four children only. Unaccompanied children are
not permitted to travel in this elevator.*

(And the same below in Chinese characters.)

He thought, "What a stupid bloody sign!" He said aloud to
the sign, 'How the hell can you be licensed to carry four children if four children aren't allowed?' He asked the sign irritably, 'Aye?' He demanded, 'Or is there some deep meaning
I'm not supposed to understand?' The elevator went up to
the fifth floor and made a *ding!* sound behind the floor number
panel above the doors. He asked the ding; 'Well?'

The doors opened onto the fifth floor and no one got in.
Auden shook his head. He asked the elevator, 'What sort of
bloody contraption is it that opens at every floor whether

7

there's someone there or not? Why the hell have call buttons on every floor if you're going to open there anyway?' He said to the elevator, 'Bloody stupid piece of machinery!'

The doors closed. The elevator carried on up to the sixth and seventh floors and then stopped. There were three more floors for the rich people, but you needed a key to make the thing travel up any higher. That pleased him. He said to the elevator that had to do as it was told, 'Ha, ha!'

The elevator's mechanism made a sighing noise and began going down again. Auden said to the elevator, 'Six!'

The doors opened on the sixth floor and no one got in.

The doors closed.

Auden said, 'Now five,' and the elevator doors opened at the fifth floor, found no one waiting and closed again. Auden said, 'Ha, ha!'

Auden said, 'Now four.'

The doors opened on four.

No one.

The doors closed.

The elevator went down.

Auden said, 'Go on, now let's see you do your magic trick.'

The elevator light showed 3 and made a *ding!*

Auden said, 'Go on then—'

The doors did not open. The elevator clicked.

Nothing.

It clicked again.

Auden said, 'Ha, bloody ha.'

Click, click, click—

Auden said, 'Ha, ha, ha, ha!'

The elevator gave up and moved downwards towards the second floor.

Auden said to the elevator, 'Ha, ha!' He said happily, 'You can't do it, can you?' He said, 'Ha! Ha! Ha!'

He felt better. He turned slightly in the car and kicked the rear wall with the toe of his shoe. He said, 'Ha, ha, ha!' He said happily, 'Stupid bloody elevator!'

The doors opened on the second floor and no one got in.

In the storeroom of P. P. Fan, Money Changers Limited of Wyang Street, Hong Bay (and other branches), Detective Inspector William Spencer sat waiting for robbers. He was happy. Of all he surveyed—which was little enough in the unlit room—he was lord: the piles of unwashed and empty money sacks marked *P. P. Fan Limited*, the piles of roneoed exchange rate sheets marked *P. P. Fan Limited* on which he sat, the Winchester 1400 20 gauge shotgun marked *Royal Hong Kong Police* which leant against the wall, and the walkie-talkie marked *Yellowthread Street Station* with which, at the flick of an aerial, he could call upon the reserves of Constable Yan parked across the street which, for the sake of anonymity, was not marked at all.

Spencer was happy. He picked up the walkie-talkie and flicked out its switch-knife aerial.

Constable Yan's voice said, 'Sir?' and waited for instructions.

Spencer cleared his throat. 'Just checking.' Spencer thought, "The essence of good stakeout procedure is to stay in constant contact with your subordinates." He said, 'Just checking.'

Yan's voice said, 'Nothing here.' He sounded a little bored. He said in Cantonese, 'Just people going about their business.'

Spencer moved slightly on the mound of exchange rates. He said back in Cantonese, 'Just keep your eyes peeled, that's all.' He leaned forward and opened the door of the storeroom a few inches to see into Mr Fan's shop. Except for Mr Fan counting money behind his counter, the shop was empty. He pressed the send button on the walkie-talkie in again and reminded Yan, 'This is good information.'

'Yes, sir.'

Spencer said, 'There are three of them, possibly Northern Chinese in origin, about five foot nine tall.'

Yan said, 'Yes.'

'Once they turn into here I want you to sing out so I'll know to expect them.' He said, 'I'll do the rest.'

9

Yan said, 'Sir.' He made a noise that sounded like a yawn being stifled.

'I won't have any warning if you don't tell me. They don't come into money changers' shouting "Your money or your life!" you know. They come in and rob the place without a sound.' He said, 'They ignore everything the victim says to them.' He asked Yan efficiently, 'Right?' He said, 'Over.'

There was a pause and then the sound of the stifled yawn again. Yan said evilly, 'Is that why they're called the deaf and dumb gang, sir?' He said, after another pause and a yawn, 'Over.'

Spencer said automatically, 'Ye—' He changed his mind. Constable Yan said, 'Sir?'

Spencer said brusquely, 'Out.'

He flicked the aerial back in.

Auden said to the lift, 'Stupid bloody elevator!' The elevator on the third floor with the doors staying shut, went *click!* *click!* *click!*

Auden said to the elevator, 'Stupid bloody machine!'

The elevator gave up and travelled upwards towards the fourth floor.

In the Detectives' Room of the Yellowthread Street Police Station, Hong Bay, Detective Chief Inspector Harry Feiffer said to Senior Detective Inspector Christopher Kwan O'Yee of the infamous Patent Exploding Radiator, 'Why don't you just put in a chit for a new one?'

O'Yee sniffed. He leaned back on his haunches on the floor of the room and patted his Exploding Radiator to console it. The radiator made a gurgling noise and sent up a sheet of flame. O'Yee said patiently, 'I have put in a chit for a new one. I put in a chit for a new one when the old one stopped working. I put in a chit asking Stores to take the old one away and give us a new one. They took the old one away.' He said huffishly, 'If it wasn't for the fact that I denied my own family the additional warmth and comfort of this, their private radiator, we, the guardians of law and order, would have ice on our arses.' The radiator spewed a gush of evil black smoke and made a grinding noise like a sand-filled carburettor. 'You've done nothing all morning but sit there and hurt its feelings.' He patted the radiator again and it calmed down, 'See?'

Feiffer took off his coat and made flapping movements with his arms to cool his armpits. 'You do realise, of course, that while it's cold, dank, misty and horrible outside, in here it's approximately one hundred and ten degrees Fahrenheit?' He glanced at the heater anxiously, 'Mind you, that's only when the bloody thing is actually working. When it isn't, it's like the Arctic on a chilly night.' He said soothingly, 'I do realise the enormous sacrifice you and your family have made, Christopher, and the deep wellsprings of generosity that prompted you to donate such a wonder of engineering to a place and people so unworthy, but do you think you could possibly get the damn thing to make up its mind one way or the other?' He said sweetly, 'I thought all you Americans were whizzes with technology. You know, the pioneering spirit of improvisation and all that—'

O'Yee looked at him.

Feiffer said, 'Have I said something wrong?'

O'Yee shook his head. He was a Eurasian, an amalgam of San Francisco and Hong Kong. It was centrally heated in San Francisco. The better class of San Franciscans, during the pioneering era, always imported their machines, craftsman-made, from Europe. O'Yee said, 'No.'

'What have I said wrong?' The radiator let off a sunspot corona of fire and missed O'Yee's eyebrows by two inches. Feiffer said, 'We could always get an engineer of some sort in to have a look at it.' He asked placatingly, 'I mean, it always works for you at home, doesn't it? Maybe it's the change of environment or something—'

O'Yee said, 'Tell me about your skeleton.'

Feiffer watched the radiator warily. He could see the whole

of Hong Bay going up in a single flash of kerosene. 'Or maybe someone from the Fire Brigade. They know quite a lot about appliances and, ah—' The radiator made a fizzing noise and he got ready to duck behind the thin protection of his Government Issue, Radiators, Exploding, Not Suitable for Protection From, Desk, and asked, 'What do you think? Would you be hurt if I—'

O'Yee fixed him with one of his sniffing looks. O'Yee sniffed.

Feiffer said, 'You'd be hurt.'

O'Yee said evenly, 'This morning, at approximately 6.25 a.m. a citizen of this community, to wit, one sampan owner/pilot, female, reported the discovery of one complete skeleton floating about the typhoon shelter on an obviously home-made raft. Upon this said raft the said person reported she also discovered a number of objects including ten sweet potatoes, a full set of dentures, a dead fish, what appeared to be a vampire's tooth, and a rope coiled around said skeleton's ankles terminating in a small length of blue drainpipe. I know, because I took the call. You, O Ungrateful One, fitting your deerstalker hat firmly between your pipe and magnifying glass, sallied forth to investigate said strange mystery. You have now returned. I therefore ask—strictly and humbly as a junior colleague—for a short résumé on your findings.'

Feiffer said, 'You *are* hurt.' He said, 'It's a lovely radiator and I apologise.' He said, 'It was a joke.'

O'Yee said pugnaciously, 'What was!'

'The skeleton! No, the *skeleton* was a joke.'

'Oh.' O'Yee turned back to the radiator, his duty done, never to communicate again.

Feiffer said, 'No, it was there all right, but according to the Government M.O. it was a student's prank.' He said with an unsuccessful attempt at levity, 'No deerstalker needed. It was a demonstration skeleton from a medical school or a doctor's office. I thought at first it might be real because there didn't appear to be any accession number on it—anatomical specimens have them, as you know—'

O'Yee said icily, 'I didn't know as a matter of fact.'

'—but the M.O. pointed out that they could be rubbed out with acetone. I suppose that's what happened. He sent the thing along to someone called Dawson at the Police Lab, but it's just—'

O'Yee looked up from his sulk. He said, interested, 'Dawson Baume?'

'Do you know him?'

'Do you?'

Feiffer said, 'No! No! No, I don't know him.' He said in an orgy of self-depreciation, 'All I know about him is that he's supposed to be the Pathologist Next To God, that he plays postal chess with Russian Grand Masters, and that he's a bit odd.'

'That's right.'

'What is?'

'That he's a bit odd.' O'Yee said, 'He's more than a bit odd. Dawson is the happy phantom of the Hong Bay Mortuary. He actually lives there. He doesn't like bodies and skeletons unless they've got a South American poison dart sticking out of them, their heads on upside down and ten toes on each hand—and a good, exotic, totally mysterious mortal injury.'

Feiffer said, 'This one didn't appear to have any injuries at all.' He said, 'It had a finger missing, but I don't suppose that counts.'

O'Yee said dismissively, 'No.'

'No.'

O'Yee said, 'He'll take one look at the wires, snort, identify the exact room in the Northern Hemisphere the thing came from, and then probably throw it straight back into the M.O.'s face.' He leaned forward and inspected the glowing wick-heart of his radiator. It seemed happy.

Feiffer said, 'What wires?'

'The wires holding it together.'

'What wires holding it together?' Feiffer said apologetically, 'My goodness me, but it's cosy in here. What a good radiator that is.' He wiped a shower of perspiration from his forehead surreptitiously.

'It is, isn't it? It's none of your cheap rubbish, this one. It's the fully adjustable model.' He said lovingly, 'It cost a fortune.' He said, 'The wires holding it together.' He patted his radiator with a congratulatory hand, 'All medical skeletons are wired together to stop them falling to pieces when the demonstrator holds them up. That's how you can tell it's a medical specimen. If it was a real skeleton then it wouldn't have had any wires and all the bits and pieces on the raft with it might have had some significance: the potatoes and the drainpipe and all the rest of it.' He glanced with affection at the smoothly functioning machine, 'In which case, you'd have something on your hands that'd make Auden's elevator door job look like Nursery Time With Lassie.' He paused, one thermal connoisseur to another, 'They don't make these radiators any more, you know.'

Feiffer did not reply.

'In a few years, they'll be collector's items.' He said, 'See this flame guard above the wick? That's hand made. You can't just turn something like that out on a stamping machine.' He turned back and decided to forgive Feiffer for his ignorance, 'It's all made by craftsmen, this.'

'There weren't any wires.'

'What?'

'There weren't any wires.'

'None at all? Or holes where at one time wires had—'

'Nothing.' Feiffer said very quietly, 'Hell, Christopher . . .'

'You don't mean you—'

Feiffer said for the second time, 'Bloody—*hell*!'

Auden travelled sourly from the sixth floor to the fifth. He thought, "This is bloody Charlie Chan stuff." He thought, "Five people have been mugged in this elevator in the past five days. All from the top three floors, all well-off, all attacked on the third floor. Five people have come down in this elevator from the top three floors in the last five days and been

14

bashed and robbed when the elevator doors opened for the third floor." He thought, "And as far as anyone can tell, the doors on the third floor have never opened from the day the building was put up eight years ago." He said to the elevator wall, 'So how the hell does someone from outside get an elevator door to open that doesn't open, mug someone inside, and then get the door closed without it ever opening in the first place? The rich buggers on the top three floors had the doors nailed shut after the first mugging. The nails are still in. How the hell does anyone go through solid wood and steel into an elevator? He thought, "Someone waits for the elevator to stop at the third floor with someone rich on board, somehow gets the door open without the passenger even noticing, and then wham! And it is the third floor because everyone who got mugged *remembers* that it was the third." He asked the elevator doors, 'So how is it done? What the hell am *I* supposed to do?' He asked the elevator, 'Aye?!' He thought, "I'm riding bloody shotgun on a goddamned stupid elevator and just what the hell am I supposed to do?" The elevator stopped at the third floor. Auden waited for it to open.

It didn't.

Auden said to the elevator, 'Go on then—open!!'

The elevator didn't. It sighed and went on up to the fourth floor.

Auden said to the elevator in disgust, 'Charlie fucking Chan!'

The elevator kept its secrets.

Auden said—

The elevator ignored him.

P. P. Fan finished counting his money and glanced nervously at the storeroom door near the front entrance of his shop. Outside, through the traffic he could see an unmarked police car that looked like nothing else in the world but an unmarked police car parked illegally on the other side of the road with an equally obvious unmarked policeman in it, reading a newspaper. P. P. Fan shook his head. In the street, a traffic warden lying doggo behind a pick-up truck moved carefully from concealment and double-timed it on rubber-soled shoes to the further concealment of a (legally) parked Land Rover. Crouched down, he inched his eyes along the bonnet and, squinting, worked out a line of advance on the unmarked police car.

P. P. Fan sighed. The door of the storeroom was open a fraction of an inch and he peered at it for the sight of twin detective's eyes watching him. The eyes did not seem to be there.

The parking warden glanced around. He drew his book of tickets from his tunic pocket in readiness and moved out onto the road and merged with the oncoming traffic.

P. P. Fan looked for the eyes. The eyes were not there. P. P. Fan said, *'Psst!'* The storeroom door, eyeless, stayed slightly open. P. P. Fan thought, "He's probably gone to sleep."

The parking warden found another car with good conceal-ment within range and sheltered behind it. He cast anxious rat-like looks behind him to make sure the coast was clear, then fixed his gaze firmly on the unmarked car. He moved forward. He only needed one more parking citation to fill his entire month's quota. This was it. He checked to make sure there was no opposition. He moved forward cautiously.

Outside Mr Fan's shop, a tall Latin-looking man stopped and watched the traffic warden in action. The tall man nodded to Mr Fan. Mr Fan nodded back.

The warden moved forward to one side of the offending vehicle. The owner/driver was reading a Chinese language newspaper with obvious illegal nonchalance and glancing over at the tall Latin watching the parking warden in the execution of his duty.

The tall Latin looked into Mr Fan's shop and then back at the traffic warden. He smiled.

P. P. Fan hissed to the detective in the storeroom, 'Psst!' The detective in the storeroom was obviously out cold. Mr Fan said, 'PSST!'

The tall Latin was a man Mr Fan had dealt with before: something intricate to do with gold coming in and going out of Macao for certain non-taxable foreign currency funding the movement of which might be facilitated if, for a large consideration, Mr Fan might like to . . . Mr Fan hissed, 'PSST!!'

The traffic warden pounced. The tall Latin looked into Mr Fan's shop and smiled again. Mr Fan began making complicated mental calculations on loss of commission on overseas Portuguese gold dealings at the current U.S. and Swiss rates of—

The traffic warden drew in a breath and said, 'Got you!'

Constable Yan lifted his warrant card a little above the level of the newspaper. 'Fuck off!' He glanced significantly at the money-changer's.

The traffic warden's mouth said, 'What—?' The tall Latin smiled again.

Constable Yan said, 'Diu ne la mo!' His tone said that after that the traffic warden could try it on his father as well.

Spencer's voice over the walkie-talkie in Yan's car said, 'Everything quiet?'

The traffic warden said, 'Oh.' He said to Yan, 'Sorry, sir.'

Spencer's voice said, 'Have you spotted someone?'

'A traffic warden.'

Spencer said in Cantonese, 'Tell him to go away.'

'I have.' Yan said to the traffic warden with the button on the walkie-talkie still on SEND, 'Go away, please.' He glanced across at the money-changer's, but there was only an innocent-looking bystander standing there. He said to the traffic warden with the button still down, 'Kindly go away inconspicuously.'

The traffic warden stiffened. He saw Yan's silver buttons under his coat. He was almost a police officer himself. He said, 'Sir!!' and saluted.

The tall Latin outside Mr Fan's establishment tensed. He turned and looked into Mr Fan's establishment at Mr Fan. Mr Fan smiled wanly at him.

The tall Latin left the area at top speed.

The European detective's eyes peered out from the open

storeroom door. The eyes looked very eager to please. The mouth below the eyes said eagerly, 'It's O.K., it was just a traffic warden.' He said encouragingly, 'No damage done.'

Mr Fan nodded his head. He said weakly. 'Thanks.'

He thought of the mouths of his starving children and could have wept.

Auden thought, "It has to be a resident because the doorman on the ground floor had orders not to admit anyone else. If it's a resident sooner or later he has to use this elevator because it's the only one in the building." He thought, "And sooner or later I'll confront him in the scene of his crime, or I'll get lucky and catch him in the act." He thought, "Brilliant." He thought, "Sooner or later the mugger will make a mistake and try to mug me." He thought, "All the muggings happen during the day, so if I ride up and down every day for a month, he'll be forced to have a go at *me*." He thought, "Brilliant."

There was a little metal sign above the emergency telephone on the rear wall. It said, in English and Chinese, PLEASE MIND YOUR HEAD. You would have had to be walking out backwards to have seen it.

He said to the elevator as it stuck for the umpteenth time on the third floor, 'I must be out of my bloody mind!'

The elevator went up to the fourth floor. With a *ding*! the elevator doors opened and someone got in.

Feiffer's phone rang. It was Dawson Baume ringing from the Morgue. Baume said, 'I've examined your skeleton.'

'And?'

Dawson Baume said, 'And it's a murder.'

He hung up.

2

There was a skylight directly above the stainless steel examination table in the centre of the mortuary room, and, hanging down from it, a single bright light. The bright light illuminated nothing but the stainless steel table and reflected the opaque outline of the skylight in the polished metal.

Against one side of the wall of the room there was a row of refrigerators, also made out of stainless steel, and, by them, a device for raising and lowering stainless steel body trays to the various layers inside the stainless steel refrigerators. The hanging light swung very slightly in an intangible breeze above the table, and from the refrigerator complex there was a steady, soft humming. There was a drainhole at the end of the stainless steel table and blood troughs running up and down both sides and, on it, laid out full-length, the skeleton.

Feiffer looked at it. The room was very cold. He said curiously, 'It looks more real.' He said, 'I suppose you accept it as real here because you expect to see a skeleton in a mortuary.' He glanced at Dawson Baume, a slight Baptist-looking man wearing steel-rimmed spectacles, and said uncomfortably, 'It didn't look that real on the raft.' He said, 'I'm sure you know the feeling.'

Dawson's face was unlined and smooth. To one side of the table was the instrument room. He turned away and went to a shelf inside it to get an instrument, the long rubber apron he wore over his clothes making a rustling sound as he walked. Feiffer asked, 'Did you make any sense of the bits and pieces that were found with it?'

'No. And it's a him, not an it.' He found the instrument and held it up in the half light to check something, 'You can tell the sex by, among other things, the size of the skull and the sacrum. And the coccyx.' He nodded his satisfaction at the state of the instrument—it was something that resembled a hand-operated dentist's drill—put it back on the shelf, and came back to the table. 'The general characteristics are European Nordic. I suppose you find the notion of a skeleton being a dead human being rather remote.' He looked down at it like an owl through the thick lenses of his glasses. 'Of course you do.' He said to himself thoughtfully, 'Hmm . . .' He put his flattened palm through the empty rib cage and made a flapping motion with it, 'See, nothing but thin air.' He withdrew his hand and said again, 'Hmmm . . .'

'You said on the phone that you had reason to believe it was a murder. Why?'

Except for his fingers, Dawson looked about thirty. The fingers were wrinkled and octogenarian and boney, like a nineteenth century print of a Dickensian undertaker. He sighed. 'There was a minute amount of brain tissue adhering to the interior of the skull in the approximate area of the lower lobes of the right cerebral hemisphere presenting certain characteristics of a skidding abrasion. There was also a minute depressed fracture approximately three inches from the centre of the cranium above the frontal lobe. Indicating a minor violent blow by an object of the approximate size of a golf ball. The skidding abrasion on the tissue indicates a violent and sudden rotation of the brain, resulting in almost instantaneous death. There were no other recent injuries to the bone structure except for the loss of the little finger on the left hand after death and the signs of an old simple fracture to one of the tarsal bones of the ankle.' He said in summary, 'Indicating that the deceased met death via a violent blow to the top of the skull by a flat object with a circular knob or protrusion attached to it at one end.' He said with a trace of professional distaste: 'Evidently, the Governor Medical Officer failed to notice any of it.' He stifled a sigh.

'How long had he been in the water?'

'Neither the body nor the skeleton had ever been immersed in either fresh or salt water for any measurable time immediately before or after death. Or recently.' He said like a witness giving evidence in Court, 'The deceased was put on the raft while he was in the state he is now and was in contact with salt water for no more than five hours. Samples of the fabricated wood from the raft suggest it to have been approximately the same *post-mortem* age as the skeleton—'

'Which is ?'

'The age of the skeleton is about thirty to forty years.'

'That's how long ago he died?'

'That's how old he was *when* he died.'

'Then how long ago did he die?'

'He died twenty years ago.' Dawson said, 'As I was about to say, the age of the raft wood in its manufactured form is also about twenty years.' He paused and raised his hand to stop Feiffer asking the next obvious question, 'However, samples of the nails used to fix the wood of the raft together examined by Forensic show them to be less than *two* years old.' He said, as a matter of fact, 'The sweet potatoes are fresh, as, relatively speaking, was the dead fish—' He said in a slightly bored tone, 'Which was gulleted by the way—a fact everyone seems to have been too busy or careless to notice— and the false teeth are locally made. An examination of the composition and type of gold in a cosmetic filling in the right incisor shows it to be of local origin.' He sighed, 'And I happen to know that the particular type of plastic based denture material used in the plates hasn't been in use since the end of the nineteen fifties.' He stifled another sigh and glanced for no particular reason at the dirty skylight, 'I happen to have trained as a dentist before I went on to medicine.' He said by way of explanation, 'A lot of people do it.' He asked, 'Anything else?'

'The rope found around the skeleton's ankles?'

'Put there after death. Poor quality hemp of no particular type or designation. The sort of thing you can find anywhere.'

He said warningly, 'I don't do drainpipes and I have no theory as to why it should be painted blue other than the simple presumption that it was painted blue because it wasn't painted green.' He said to Feiffer, 'I don't expect you people take skeletons too seriously anyway.' He sounded very world-weary. He glanced down at the table.

'If it didn't come from the sea, where did it come from?'

'It came from the ground. Residues left from the decomposition process that defleshed it show it to have been buried undisturbed for approximately twenty years in sandy ground. There's no evidence of nitrates other than the norm so it's possible that it wasn't buried in artificially fertilised agricultural land.'

Feiffer said, 'The budgets of impecunious farmers in Hong Kong don't usually run to artificial fertilisers.'

'No?'

'No.'

Dawson said, 'I didn't know that. In that case, it might have been.' He asked, 'What do you propose to do?'

'I propose to identify it.'

Dawson said wearily, 'Him.'

'Him then. By the dentures if they're locally made.'

'They are.'

'Then that's what I propose to do.' He glanced at the skeleton, 'Provided there are no other more pressing matters to be dealt with.'

'Sure.'

'In any event, if, as you say, he's been in the ground for at least twenty years then another few—'

Dawson said, 'That's right.' He asked, 'How tall are you, Mr Feiffer?'

'About five foot eleven. Why?'

Dawson said, 'So was he. I guess your age to be about forty. He was maybe eight or nine years younger.' He asked 'Are you married?'

'Yes.'

Dawson said, 'Maybe he was too.' He said, 'At one stage,

he limped. At one time he broke his ankle and there must have been people who were sorry for him and said as the break mended, "It's getting a lot better." And he must have turned around and said, "Yes, thanks." ' He said with a shrug, 'So what? Who cares?' He said coldly, 'In my opinion, the nature of the skull fracture and the internal brain abrasions lead me to believe that he was probably killed from behind by a blow from a flat shovel. The golf ball fracture could be the little knob where the blade meets the handle. After that, who-ever did it probably used the shovel to bury him. As to who dug him up again and set him adrift on a raft, I have no idea—nor any idea how to find out.'

Feiffer said, 'The tide charts would probably indicate the launching point.'

Dawson said, 'If anyone was interested enough to find out.' He asked, 'Or are tide charts just part of the routine?'

'It is routine procedure, yes.'

'Oh.' Dawson nodded. He glanced down at the skeleton. 'Anything else?' He turned to go back to the instrument room.

'Not that I can think of.'

'Hmm. I'll be back in a moment. If you like you can cover him up with that sheet.' He said again, 'Hmm . . .'

He went into the instrument room and closed the door.

There was a faint sound of the wind outside the stone walls of the Mortuary examination room and, on the specimen jars and bottles lined up on a wooden shelf in the light from the bulb, a layer of thick dust. Feiffer glanced down at the outline of the skeleton. Covered up with a sheet, it looked as though there was a real person under there with flesh and a face, eyes and appearance. There wasn't. It was just a collection of twenty-year-old bones. There was an antiseptic smell on the floor, lysol, and a coldness that meant that nothing warm and alive lived in the room. The thing below the sheet was very still. It had been dead for decades.

Feiffer thought, "The difference is that it's extinct." He thought, "There's no connection between it and a real person,

23

nothing human about it that strikes a chord." He thought, "It takes an effort of will to realise that it was once someone who walked around."

He thought, "With a limp." He thought, "At one time he had a broken ankle."

He glanced at the instrument room door, but it was closed tight.

He thought, "I suppose he must have gone to a hospital or a doctor to have it set. Odd to think that people did things for a collection of bones." He thought, "It wasn't a collection of bones then. There was a dressed body encasing the bones and the dressed body did things and said things." He thought, "But I just can't bring myself to feel any connection between the thing under the sheet and a human being—there just isn't any real connection." The outline under the stark white sheet looked like it had never had the motive power to make the sheet move—to make it rise and fall rhythmically with the gentle, steady, unstopping motion of its lungs. "You look at it and there's no sense of the loss of life. You look at it and it's so remote that there's no feeling of regret and—that it could have done more things if it had lived." He thought, "There are more pressing things to do than waste time on something that looks like it should be in a glass case in a museum."

He walked over to the shelf of pickled specimens, lit a cigarette, and began reading the faded labels.

The labels were all in Latin.

Auden scrutinised the someone who had got into the elevator on the fourth floor. The someone was a middle-aged man, reasonably respectable. The middle-aged man scrutinised him.

Auden said in Cantonese, 'I'm a police officer.' The elevator doors closed.

The middle-aged man looked at him.

'You knew that already.'

The middle-aged man looked at him.

'Didn't you?'

24

The middle-aged man looked at him.

Auden said, 'Of course you did. I could tell.' He said, 'Don't be concerned. I'd just like to ask you a few questions about the muggings. All right?'

The middle-aged man nodded. He looked a little confused.

Auden said pleasantly, 'You didn't think I was the mugger, did you?'

The middle-aged man looked wary. He shook his head.

Auden said, 'Fine.' He stretched back against the corner of the elevator and made ready to put a few searching questions. He said searchingly, 'O.K?'

The middle-aged man nodded.

Auden said, 'Right. Here we go then—'

The middle-aged man said, 'What mugger?'

Feiffer glanced at his watch. The instrument room door was still closed and if Dawson was doing something in there, he was being very quiet about it.

Feiffer glanced at the outline of the skeleton on the table. He thought, "It's possible that he's wrong about the dentures. For all he really knows, they could be positively ancient. A real, practising dentist will take one look at them and realise they're forty or fifty years old." He remembered the vampire's tooth and thought he had better ask Dawson about that too, then thought, "To hell with it, I'll ask a real dentist and it'll turn out to be a piece of rock or something." He went towards the instrument room door to knock up Dawson and thought, "That's what I'll do." He thought, "This fellow Dawson is just odd. The skeleton will turn out to be someone who was killed in the War." He bumped into the steel table and dropped ash from his cigarette onto the sheet at the head end.

He said without thinking, 'Sorry.'

He stopped.

He said to the outline under the sheet, 'I must be losing my mind.' He brushed the ash away with the heel of his hand and felt, under the sheet, the outline of the head. He said aloud, 'Skull, not head.' He thought, "You limped. At one time you broke your ankle and you limped." He thought, "And one day when it was healing you found you could get your sock over it and someone standing there watching you said, 'Hey—well done!' and you smiled at them." He thought, "This is crazy!"

He thought, "And you had flesh on your arms and you wore a watch and carried money and had keys and bits of old tramtickets. And when you went missing, someone was worried."

He thought, "What if you were me?" He said to the outline under the sheet, 'What if it was me?'

They were the same height. Feiffer thought, 'What if it was me?"

He brushed another speck from the sheet very gently and said to the outline, 'It's this place and the silence.' There was still another speck. He flicked it away with his finger and rubbed the mark clean. "What if he did die recently and he wasn't just a casualty from the war?" He thought, "It's understandable in a war. You expect to be bumped off when there are people around with guns. It's decisive and finished and explicable." He thought, "But what if, in an instant, for a reason you never knew, you were killed for nothing?" He had a picture in his mind of the flashing edge of a shovel coming down in a blur of light and connecting with something hard. "And what if you weren't fully dead when whoever did it began digging up the ground to cover you? What if you saw their face for an instant?"

He said suddenly to the figure under the sheet, 'All right!' He said more quietly, 'All right.' He said again, 'O.K.'

He turned around. The door to the instrument room behind him was open and Dawson, wearing his long rubber apron, was standing there watching him.

Dawson said quietly, 'It was a person.'

Feiffer nodded.

Dawson said, 'It was a man.'

Feiffer said, 'Yes.'

26

Dawson nodded. 'I've just done an acid test on the other thing—on the vampire tooth.'

'And?'

'And it's a pebble of quartz.' Dawson Baume said after a moment, 'I'm very glad.'

'About what?'

Dawson said, '. . . nothing.' He shrugged his shoulders.

Feiffer said, 'I—I gather you play postal chess.'

'Yes. Do you?'

'I'm afraid not.'

Dawson shrugged again. In the poor light at the instrument room door he looked very young and unlined, like a student. 'It's not the same as the real thing.'

Feiffer said, 'No?'

'No.'

Feiffer said uncomfortably, 'Well, I'd better get on with it then. When I find out who he was, do you want me to let you know?'

'If you like. Yes.' He nodded and went to the main door of the room and slid it back for Feiffer to pass. 'Perhaps I'll see you again.' He waited until Feiffer had turned the corner outside to go to the carpark and then slid the mortuary door closed again and locked it.

When you played postal chess there were no spectators and no one to tell you whether you had done the right thing, made the right move, exposed or covered yourself. You always had to wait for the result to find out whether or not you had made a fool of yourself. He was alone. He had no one to talk to. He stopped in the centre of the room and ran his ancient hand across his mouth and wondered.

O'Yee's voice at the other end of the line said pleasantly, 'Did you meet the H.P.R.M.?'

Feiffer said, 'Who's the H.P.R.M.?'

'You know, Doctor Dawson Baume M.D., the Happy Phantom of the Rue Morgue.'

There was a bus going by the telephone box in the carpark

outside the mortuary. Feiffer waited until it passed. He said, 'I've decided we're going to make a maximum effort on this one, Christopher.'

'Why?'

Feiffer said, 'The raft was in the water for no more than a few hours. Dawson Baume seems to think about four or five. I'm going around now to the Water Police to have a chat to one of their tide and current experts to see where it came from. In the meantime, I want you to have the dental charts circulated to all the dentists and dental mechanics in the Colony.'

'The teeth from the raft?'

'Yes. I want a quick answer so you'd better have one of the uniformed men take them around to all the other Stations by car. Can you arrange that?'

O'Yee said, 'Far be it from me to question the wisdom of a superior officer, Harry, and a genuine White Man at that, but—'

Feiffer said, 'And I'll ring in for the results as soon as I've got an answer from the Water Police. O.K?'

There was a pause at the other end of the line. After a moment O'Yee said, 'If that's what you want.'

'That's what I want.'

O'Yee said, 'You still haven't told me how the erstwhile but odd Dawson struck you.'

Feiffer snapped at him, 'Just do it, will you!'

O'Yee said, 'Yes, Massa! If dat what de Massa want, den dat what de slave do!' He heard a click at the other end of the line as Feiffer hung up.

Dawson *wondered*.

—he wondered what people thought of him.

3

Now, if there was one thing P. P. Fan knew about— above all else—it was profit. He looked over at the half open door behind which an armed moron with an undeveloped commercial sense sheltered cramped and obediently to protect him and a wave of sympathy crossed (not without some difficulty) across P. P. Fan's lined and profitable face.

P. P. Fan thought, "This European with blue eyes and an uncommercial mind is in there doing his best to protect my business from robbers. Quite possibly at the risk of his own life, such as it is. As a simple business transaction if nothing else, it therefore behoves me with the full weight of my fifty-two years of varied experience to give him something in return. A little glimpse of the financial acumen that has made me what I am today would be appropriate." He thought, "The man has simply lacked the opportunities I had when I was young or he would have made his mark as something other than a lowly policeman. In his own way he's probably even a moderately bright fellow." He thought, "And, anyway, it'll give me merit in the next life doing something selfless for someone else." He nodded to himself, stopped outside the half open door, keeping an eye on the till, and said in English to the two inches of pine wood between him at the time of the fullness of his years and reminiscences and the idiot cop who frightened customers away, 'Hey, you!'

The door opened a fraction of an inch in readiness. The pair of pale blue eyes glanced anxiously back and forth. The voice said, 'I can't come out until something happens.' He asked enthusiastically, 'Has something happened?'

P. P. Fan glanced at his cash till. He drew a breath and wondered whether the merit in acts of merit was really all it was cracked up to be. He said wearily, 'No.' He asked, 'Is everything all right in there for you?'

'It's dark.'

P. P. Fan nodded.

Spencer's voice said, 'And it's a bit cold.'

'Apart from that?'

The voice did not answer. There was a loud metallic click.

P. P. Fan said, 'Be careful with that shotgun in there!'

The voice said, 'That was my knees. I've been sitting down on a pile of old papers.' The voice said, 'The shotgun isn't even loaded. I've got the cartridges in my pocket.' The voice said reassuringly, 'Don't worry about me, I'm not trigger-happy or anything.' The voice sounded as if it was coming from a child locked in a cupboard.

P. P. Fan said, 'As a matter of fact, that pile of papers is the complete list of fluctuations in the U.S. dollar exchange rate since 1929.' He said, 'That's how I got my start.' He paused, letting all the vicissitudes and victories come back to him in luxurious nostalgia, 'Did you know that the dollar buying power against the local tael in 1938 in Shanghai quadrupled during the months of June and July and then held steady until almost the end of August?' He said, 'It's all in there. It isn't just changing a few pesos into patacas for tourists, currency exchange, you know. It's much more complicated than that. You need to be aware of trends.' He said, 'Unless you want to stay as you are for the next thirty years you could do a lot worse than study all the valuable information you're resting your arse on.' He said, a trifle piqued, 'What do you think got me where I am today? *Luck*?'

There was a brief silence from inside the storeroom. The child's voice in the cupboard said softly, 'Sorry.' The voice said, 'I've gotten off the papers now.' The voice said, 'I'm squatting against the wall.'

That was better. P. P. Fan cast a quick look to the entrance of his shop. It was a quiet morning. (It always was this time of year—a quick perusal of the Shanghai day returns for any year since 1931 would show anyone that it was going to be). 'What do you want to be when you've finished this policeman thing?'

'I hadn't thought about it.' The voice said, 'I thought I'd stay on as a poli—' The voice said, anxious not to lose face, 'I hadn't really thought about it.' The voice asked, 'That's not very farseeing of me, is it?' The voice said, trying to please, 'I mean from a point of view of graphs of past and future trends—' He said, a little worried, 'I hadn't really thought about it at all. I thought I'd wait until I got married and ask my wife's advice.'

P. P. Fan shook his head. He put a long money-counting finger in his right ear and swivelled it around to remove the wax. He said, 'I must have misheard you. I thought for a moment you were saying you'd ask the advice of your *wife*—' He said, anxious not to give so great an offence, 'No one could be that stupid.' He said decisively, 'I misheard you. You said, "I'll ask for advice about my life." ' He said, 'That's what you said, wasn't it?'

'Yes!' The twin eyes flickered around and if eyes could be said to look sheepish, then those eyes did. The voice behind the yes said, 'You're absolutely right. I should get some advice.' The voice asked, 'You're fairly well-off, aren't you?'

P. P. Fan gazed heavenwards at the ceiling. 'You don't ask people that! That's the first thing to learn: that you don't ask that. They'll only lie to you.' P. P. Fan said, 'As a matter of fact, I'm deep in the straits of dire poverty.'

'Oh.' The voice paused sympathetically for a moment, 'I'm very sorry to hear that.' The voice said—

P. P. Fan said, 'I'm lying!'

'Oh!' The voice said, 'I'm glad to hear it.' It dropped to a more personal level, 'I must say, to be honest, I got the impression from your shop that you were very well off indeed—'

P. P. Fan said, 'I'm not very well off indeed!'

The voice said, 'Ha! Ha!' The voice said happily, 'I know, you're bloody *rich*!'

P. P. Fan shouted at the two-inch-thick door concealing the two-inch-thick head, 'I'm not bloody *rich*!'

The voice, getting into the swing of things, said happily, 'I know, and now you're lying again—right?'

'I'm not lying! Who says they're rich? Only lunatics who aren't rich say they're rich—' He said, 'Do you want to be hit for money by every deadbeat and criminal in the entire world?!' P. P. Fan shouted, 'I'm *comfortable*—that's all. Comfortable! Have you got that?'

There was a long silence from the storeroom while, P. P. Fan assumed, the English Bonehead in there tried to work out in his pigeon's brain whether or not that too was a lie.

P. P. Fan said, 'You're not trying to work out whether or not that was a lie too, are you?'

Pigeonbrain said, 'Oh—um, no.' There was another silence.

P. P. Fan said, 'Well what the hell *are* you doing?'

There was another silence.

P. P. Fan said, 'Well?'

Silence.

P. P. Fan despaired. He began to say—

The voice from the cupboard said very softly, 'My leg's gone to sleep.' The voice asked apologetically, 'Would you mind, really a lot, if I sat on your papers for a couple of minutes until it wakes up?'

P. P. Fan sighed a deep, despairing sigh.

'What do you mean, "What mugger?"'

The middle-aged man in the elevator looked at him sheepishly. He shrugged his shoulders.

Auden said, 'Well? What do you mean?'

The man said, 'Um . . .'

The voice from inside the dark, cold storeroom said, 'I, ah—well, I like helping people.'

32

There was no reply.

The voice said, 'That's why I wanted to be a pol
to help people.' You could tell that the voice t
sounded pretty silly. The voice asked, 'Does that sou
silly?'

P. P. Fan said, 'Yes.'

The voice said, 'I, ah, wanted to do some good—' The voice
said petulantly, 'I'm sorry that sounds silly.' It said quickly,
'I mean look at you, I'm helping you now.' The voice nodded
to itself. The voice said modestly, 'Aren't I?'

P. P. Fan said effortlessly, 'And that's why I'm helping you:
because you're so young and innocent and you sincerely
believe that you can do good.'

'Oh.' The voice said, 'Um . . . . I can do more good as a
policeman than as a tycoon.' The voice said, 'Like—like a
priest, for example.' The voice said, 'Priests are unworldly and
poor.'

P. P. Fan said, 'And they do good.'

'Right!' You could tell the voice thought it had triumphed
by the simple expedient of quoting fragments of superior
Western tradition at the poor Oriental. The voice said, 'I'm
talking about Catholic and Anglican priests—you know,
priests who—'

P. P. Fan said, 'Priests certainly do a lot of good.' He said,
'Sticking to your example of Rome, only the Vatican does
more good.' He said, 'I suppose that's because the Vatican as
a corporate identity is more powerful and able to bring more
influence to bear than any one, individual cleric.' He asked the
voice, 'Are you a Catholic, as a matter of fact?'

'No, I'm not.' The voice said, 'I'm glad you see my point.
I think that being a policeman is a vocation, like a priest or—'
The voice said patronisingly, 'Or, to put it in a Chinese con-
text—'

P. P. Fan said, '*Why* is the Vatican more powerful and
influential than an individual poverty-stricken priest?'

'Pardon?'

P. P. Fan said, 'I always thought it was because they had

33

more resources at their disposal. You know, money. Or, to put it in a Western context—'

There was a silence from the boxed-in voice.

P. P. Fan said, '*Two men seeing eye to eye,*
Having money gold can buy:
Without money, though he try,
One cannot a needle buy.'

He said, 'A little bit of Oriental sagacity practised *par excellence* in the West.' He added to fix the point, '*Nicht wahr?*' He thought, "Stick that in against your Western tradition!"

Spencer said, 'Oh.'

'*Having capital to open an eating house, I dread not the most capricious stomach. With never a single hemp thread in his hand, he thinks to make a dozen nets. Who does not ready money clutch, Of business talent has not much.* He said, 'Think on that.' He said, merciless in merit, '*From small profits and many expenses, Comes a whole life of sad consequences.*' He asked the two-inch-thick door, 'Do you realise that the pile of useless papers—to your poor mind—on which you are resting contains the key to complete business success? The key to unlock and activate the commercial mind?' He asked the door and the gods, 'Why am I so anxious to impart my secrets to you when you don't even appreciate them?'

The voice said, seizing the opening, 'Because you're trying to do good!'

'Ah-ha! And would I be in a position to do so much good if I was a poverty-striken coolie or a policeman?' P. P. Fan said, 'No!' He said, 'I rest my case.' He said, 'Think about that!' He said, in triumph, 'Well, what *do* you think?'

'Well, I'm . . . I'm . . . Well, I'm—' The voice said, 'Well I'm in your debt and, um, I, um . . .' The voice said, 'I'm very grateful for the interest you've—'

P. P. Fan said, '*The meritorious man will even lend you the plinths of his pillars. You borrow my umbrella—to thank me do not try; but through the night, I'd ask you, please, hang it up to dry.*' He added in a virtuous voice, '*Virtuous men are a kingdom's pleasure.*' He said, '*Debts unpaid are like untied corpses.*'

Spencer said, 'Oh?'

'They come back to haunt you.' P. P. Fan asked anxiously, 'Are you following all these precepts?'

'Yes!'

'Then read my secret papers and learn something useful!' P. P. Fan said, 'You are the sort of ungrateful bastard who makes acts of merit very difficult.'

The voice paused.

'That wasn't a precept. You're not supposed to hear that one in reverential silence; you're supposed to say "Sorry." '

'Sorry.'

P. P. Fan sighed a long-suffering sigh.

The voice from the storeroom said, 'I couldn't see to read in here anyway.'

P. P. Fan said, 'I'll get you a flashlight.'

'Thanks very much.'

P. P. Fan said, 'It's a pleasure.'

He went behind his counter to get the flashlight he kept for making sure the bottoms of his money sacks were absolutely empty. He thought, "By Heaven, there had better be a place for meritorious acts in the next life or someone's going to suffer!" He said to the storeroom in an undertone, 'Think nothing of it.'

Auden said suspiciously, 'Then let me explain it to you. Someone who has access to this building is going around hitting people on the head in this elevator and robbing them. O.K?'

The middle-aged man nodded.

'And he is doing it from a base on the third floor. He is waiting for the elevator to come down from the upper floors to the third floor and then, when the elevator opens at the third floor, he is leaning in and hitting them. Got that, have you?'

The man nodded.

'And then he is letting the elevator continue its journey down to the ground floor where the victim is discovered dazed and robbed by the doorman. *I* am riding up and down in this elevator in the hope of discovering how this is done. Right?'

The man looked dubious.

'Right?'

'Right! Right!'

'Further, the person in question then somehow manages to get away from the scene of the crime without anyone ever noticing him. And, further than that, there is one small complication: the doors on the third floor don't open. They haven't opened since the building was constructed, and even further, some of the upper floor residents who have already been hit and robbed in the last five days have had the third floor doors nailed up to make bloody *sure* they don't open.' Auden said, 'I have interviewed all the residents on the third floor and they say not only have they not seen anything, they haven't heard anything, and they don't know anything.' He looked at the man.

The man said, 'I don't know anything either. I live on the fourth floor myself.' He said in agreement, 'It certainly is a mystery, isn't it? How's it done?'

'I don't know how it's done. That's why I'm riding up and down in this elevator. I'm trying to find out.'

'Why don't the people who get mugged see who it is when the doors open?'

Auden said, 'Something always distracts them.'

'Just as the doors open?'

'*Yes!*'

'What?'

Auden said wearily, 'That's what I'm riding up and down in this elevator trying to find out.'

'How do they know it's the third floor?'

'Because they see the light go on on the panel and they hear the bell!'

'Maybe the robber's—'

36

Auden said, 'The wiring's been checked. It hasn't been touched.'

'Then how does the robber get the third floor doors open?'

'That's why I'm riding up and down in this bloody elevator trying to—!'

'Oh! Yes! Sorry!' The man glanced at the light panel above the door. It made a ding noise and the light came on for the seventh floor. The man said, 'This is where I get out.' He said to lighten the detective's burden, 'I'm going to see my brother who lives in apartment 73. I'm from apartment 42 on the fourth floor.' He said appreciatively, 'Well, it really is something to get your mind working, isn't it?' He said, 'I certainly hope you find the solution even if it takes you all morning.'

'Thanks very much!'

The doors opened and the man got out on the seventh floor and waited until the elevator went down to the ground.

The middle-aged man shook his head admiringly. His brother-in-law was a policeman in the Traffic Section and he had heard some of the excuses he made up so he could stop somewhere away from the action and have a few hours break. This European's story made his brother-in-law seem as though he was still in nursery. He followed the elevator lights as they flickered along the panel. The light stopped briefly on the fourth floor and then went out again as the car went up again towards the fifth.

The middle-aged man went towards his brother's apartment shaking his head. The middle-aged man thought that after this anyone who said that Europeans were a bit thick was an idiot.

The elevator doors opened on the seventh floor with a *ding*! as his brother let him into his apartment still shaking his head.

Spencer hissed into his walkie-talkie, 'I'm reading!' The U.S. dollar during the months of April, May, 1946 had moved in a very interesting falling parabola that, in a way, seemed strangely reminiscent of, in reverse, its gain during the months of September, October 1937 . . . 'Well, what do you want?' And the hardening of Thirty Day Redeemable Treasury Bonds against both the Swiss franc and the West German mark during the era of the Cold War confrontation of . . . well, if you considered the state of exchange in February 1938 against . . .

In the car outside, Constable Yan shook his walkie-talkie to get Detective Inspector Spencer back on the air again. He said, 'Sir? Mr Spencer?'

'What? What!'

'Is everything all right?'

'Yes, *yes*! How's everything out there?'

'Fine. So far there's been no sign of any—'

'Good. Over and out!'

'—sir? Mr Spencer!'

'*What?*'

Constable Yan said, 'Um, is-everything-all-right-in-there? You-are-not-feeling-lonely, are you? Mr-Spencer?'

'What—?'

'The-numerous-employees-of-the-business-are-all-in-there-with-you-are-they?'

Spencer's voice said, 'I'm trying to concentrate!'

'Is-everyone—'

Spencer shouted across the airwaves, 'Are you trying to be funny?'

'It's a code!' Yan said, 'I was using a code in case you were being held captive by criminals and you couldn't speak freely.' He said, 'It didn't sound like you so I—'

'It didn't sound like me because I'm trying to concentrate!' Spencer's voice said uncharacteristically testily, 'I can't afford to stay a dumb policeman *all* my life! I've got to better myself.' He said, 'O.K?' There was a pause and then, in his old voice, Spencer's voice said, 'I'm sorry I snapped at you, I'm just trying to concentrate on something a bit difficult, that's all. Is everything quiet out there?'

'Everything.'

'Good. That's fine. Great. Thanks very much for being so alert.' He asked pleasantly, 'Is there anything else?'

Yan said warily, 'Look, if there's anything wrong in there I can—'

'There's nothing wrong!' (Well, that blew any hope of seeing a firm predictable movement in the dollar to deutschmark ratio for 1953) 'By the way, tell Mr Feiffer that the rope around the skeleton's ankles is to stop the spirit coming back again.' He added, 'Probably an old peasant superstition.' He said airily, 'Just a snippet I picked up from a business associate. O.K?'

Constable Yan said, 'O.K! Well done!'

'You can have the credit if you like—I don't need it.' There was a rustling sound behind his voice, like papers being shuffled, 'O.K?'

Constable Yan said, 'Right!' He said, 'Thanks very much.'

'Hmm.' The magnate of the Far East said airily, 'Consider it a trifle.' He went back to his reading as, outside P. P. Fan's shop, an armed criminal intent on the redistribution by force of Mr Fan's amassed wealth, decided to get on with it.

Sergeant Lew of the Water Police leaned forward over his tide and current charts of the South China Coast. He glanced at Feiffer and took up an expanding compass and calibrated it against the printed scale at the bottom of the first map. 'A wooden raft?'

Feiffer nodded.

Lew screwed up his eyes. He was a squat uniformed man in his early forties and he had the look of the Hong Kong boat people about him. 'Launched when?'

'It was discovered on the beach at about 7 in the morning—'

Lew said, 'High tide was at 6.21.'

'And according to the evidence from Forensic it had been immersed in salt water for about four to five hours—'

'So we can assume it was launched at approximately two o'clock in the morning?'

'Yes.'

Sergeant Lew consulted his charts and impaled his compass in the centre of a totally blank spot in the South China Sea. He swivelled the instrument and used the point of it to describe an arc along a section of the coast in the Hong Bay District. Lew said, 'It was launched somewhere there.'

'Here in Hong Bay?'

'Probably from the vicinity of one of the waterfront market gardens along Hop Pei Cove. Does that make sense?'

'It does if it's an old market garden custom to rope the ankles of corpses together to stop them coming back to haunt you. Is it?'

'I don't know.' Sergeant Lew said, 'I'm not from farming people. My family comes from Tanka fishing stock. But it wouldn't surprise me to hear that peasants did things like that.' He said gratefully, 'Peasants have never interested me.' He asked out of mild academic curiosity about the lesser breeds, 'Where did you hear it anyway?'

'One of my Constables evidently thought of it.'

'Then my estimate that the raft came from a farm was a good one.'

'Yes.'

Sergeant Lew shrugged. Nothing to a man born and bred in the clear salt sea air of the fishing grounds. He said, 'I'm not saying I know anything about the miserable lives of farmers, but I gather from conversations I may have accidentally over-heard from time to time that sweet potatoes are only grown in the New Territories and Kowloon, hardly ever on the Hong Kong island itself.' He shrugged. 'So if the potatoes found on the raft came from a farm here on Hong Kong it shouldn't be too hard to locate it.' He said, 'If I were you, I'd go and have a talk to someone at the Vegetable Growers' and Market Gardeners' Association in Tiger Snake Road.' He said off-handedly, 'Maybe they could help you. From what you've mentioned about the gulleted fish it'd fit in. A *Priacanthus Niphonius* is a trash fish otherwise called the Japanese Big-Eye.' He said casually, 'Only a landman peasant farmer would actually go to the trouble of gulleting and eating

40

something like that.' He smiled to himself. 'Try the Vegetable Association if you want to find out exactly which farm it came from.'

Feiffer said, 'Thank you very much indeed.'

Sergeant Lew smiled. 'It's a pleasure. Always glad to help.' He waved his hand. 'It's all a nice, pleasant, slow-motion loaf if I may say so, sir. And very well deserved.'

'What is?'

Sergeant Lew smiled. He wasn't one to puncture someone else's pretended duty, 'This skeleton business.' He grinned. 'If I'd found it I probably would have chucked it straight back into the drink.' He glanced at Feiffer's face. He said wearily, 'Have I said something wrong?'

The Chinese Desk Constable at the door of the Water Police building said, 'Chief Inspector Feiffer?'

'Yes.'

The Desk Constable held up a telephone.

It was O'Yee. O'Yee said, 'Now I can't get it to go out. It's like an inferno in here.' He said, 'Hang on a sec.' He shuffled some papers, 'I've got a report in from the dental mechanic who made the false teeth. They were made in North Point in 1954 for an American.'

'Name?'

'George Edward Putnam. Any idea yet where he came from?'

'Probably a market garden growing sweet potatoes somewhere in the Hop Pei Cove area.'

'Really?'

'Address?'

'The dentist didn't have it. He paid cash. He may have been a local resident.'

Feiffer said, 'If he was a Hong Kong resident we've got records on him. If he was an American, then the Americans have got records on him.'

'Only if he was in the Services or committed a crime. It isn't Russia yet.' O'Yee said, 'I'll get moving on it.'

'Fine.'

'Harry—?'

'What?'

O'Yee said softly, 'What the devil was an American named George Edward Putnam doing in a sweet potato farm in Hop Pei Cove that caused him to float into a typhoon shelter on a raft twenty years later as a skeleton with his skull bashed in?'

Feiffer said irritably, 'That's what I'm in the process of trying to find out, isn't it?'

O'Yee said, 'Yes, Bwana! Sorry, Bwana! Thank you, Bwana!' He said, 'Hmm . . .'

He hung up.

4

Constable Yan folded his newspaper with the neurotic neatness of a policeman suffering from parked-car stakeout boredom and set it obsessionally straight on the seat next to him. A corner of the folded tabloid hung over the edge of the leatherette and he flicked it with his finger and set it right. Now a corner against the back of the seat was out of true. He touched the corner carefully with the same finger—keeping one suspicious eye on the original edge—and set the whole rectangle of newsprint minutely right. He gazed at the arrangement critically and decided the whole thing would look better the other way around. He glanced across to the money-changer's premises and wondered why detectives always took anonymous tip-offs seriously. There was a Chinese youth wearing a sports coat and dark trousers in the shop. The youth carried an unmarked airline bag. Constable Yan moved the newspaper the other way around and surveyed it thoughtfully. He turned his head back to the shop to see what the youth was doing. The youth reached into the bag and took out something to assist in the money-changing rigmarole. Constable Yan yawned. The youth took out the object and looked at it for a moment. It was a sawn-off rifle. The youth pointed it at P. P. Fan.

Yan reached for the walkie-talkie and flicked out the aerial. Yan said, 'Sir—!'

A voice said irritably, 'Shh!' It was the Concentrating Spencer.

Yan said, 'Sir, there's a—'

'For God's sake, can't you leave me alone! I'm trying to concentrate!' The Concentrating Spencer said again, 'SHH!'

Yan said, 'Listen, there's a—' and then there was a burst of static as, at the other end, the receiver was turned off and he tried to talk to thin air. Yan glanced at the bandit in the shop and thought, "Inspector Spencer's already spotted him and he's telling me to keep quiet so the bandit won't hear." The owner of the shop was piling money into a sack. He looked as if *he* didn't think the bandit had been spotted. Yan thought, "No, he hasn't. He's missed him." He thought, "Well, I haven't!"

In the storeroom, the Concentrating Spencer pondered over the sudden and, on the surface at least, inexplicable fall of the dollar against the Italian lira in 1955. He went back to the figures for 1954 and ran his finger carefully down the column of changing numbers and thought, "Hmm . . ." then went back again to 1955 and then on to 1956. The Concentrating Spencer thought, "Odd that . . ." He thought, "Hmm, very odd . . ."

P. P. Fan looked at the bandit. The bandit moved the muzzle of the sawn-off rifle up a few inches so that P. P. Fan was looking at the muzzle. P. P. Fan swallowed and said, 'How much do you want?'

The bandit smiled at him.

P. P. Fan said incredulously, 'All of it?'

The bandit nodded.

P. P. Fan said, 'Why don't you talk?'

The bandit smiled and pointed to the muzzle with his trigger finger. The bandit said, '—Pzztt!!'

Constable Yan got across the street and squeezed between two parked cars in front of P. P. Fan's premises. From inside, the bandit glanced out at him—an anonymous looking man in a light topcoat crossing the road—and then looked back to P. P. Fan with the rifle hidden a little closer against his body.

Constable Yan unbuttoned the middle button of his topcoat.

The bandit glanced back to the street and turned and

44

nodded to P. P. Fan to hurry up with whatever he was doing with the money sacks.

P. P. Fan hurried. He cast a quick unhappy look at the storeroom.

Yan glanced back across the street. Yan thought, "I can't go in there with my revolver in my hand or he'll start shooting as soon as I get to the door. I wouldn't get a word out before he—" He thought, "Where the hell's Inspector Spencer?" He reached in through the false pocket in his topcoat to his Sam Brown belt, "I'll have to try and get in and brain him with my truncheon."

He went into the money-changer's.

P. P. Fan looked up. His eyes widened. He looked at the bandit. The bandit's eye began to travel with the muzzle of the sawn-off rifle towards the door. P. P. Fan said desperately, 'Why don't you speak?' The bandit saw the anonymous top-coated man's hand slide inside his coat.

P. P. Fan said, 'Why don't you say something?' as the bandit swivelled the muzzle towards the door and made a clicking noise somewhere near the breech of the gun.

Constable Yan said, 'Police!' He got the truncheon out cleanly from under his coat and spun it back in his hand like a baseball pitcher. The bandit's gun muzzle came up as the truncheon went flying through the air like a black bomb. The bandit said in a broad Australian accent, 'Jesus H. bloody *Christ*!' as the base of the ebony baton caught him on the temple and dropped him like a felled ox. Yan said unnecessarily, 'Police,' and went forward to retrieve first the gun and then the nightstick.

The bandit raised himself to one elbow. He looked at the gun and the truncheon and then he felt his head. His head made its presence known by a wave of throbbing. The bandit said softly to himself, '*Struth*—!' and let his head drop back onto the floor.

P. P. Fan said, 'He wanted all my money.' You could tell he thought it was a black day for Hong Kong Chinese-Australian relations.

The bandit looked at him and made a moaning sound like a Bondi tram gone off the rails.

On the phone, O'Yee's voice said, 'Wait till I shove the radiator away from the telephone.' There was a radiator-shoving sound and then a *phew*! as the shimmering heat in the Detectives' Room must have dissipated a little. O'Yee said, 'So why didn't he speak?'

'He had a broad Australian accent. I suppose he thought it'd give him away.' Spencer glanced at Yan dragging the semi-comatose bandit along the floor towards the rear of the shop and added, 'Yan's bringing him in now.'

O'Yee said in his broad West Coast accent, 'I guess it would have.' He thought about it or the radiator for a moment, 'It's good work anyway.' He said, 'I suppose the other two decided to leave it today. Lucky for them.' He asked suddenly, 'He is a member of the gang isn't he? His description fits?'

Spencer glanced unhappily at P. P. Fan. P. P. Fan was watching Constable Yan dragging with a look of satisfaction on his face. Spencer said, 'He isn't one of the deaf and dumb gang.' (P. P. Fan glanced at him with horror.) Spencer said softly, 'I have to confess, Christopher, that I didn't even see him come in. Constable Yan followed him across the street and got him with his truncheon.' Spencer said quickly, 'I'm afraid I had nothing to do with it at all.'

There was no reply.

Spencer said, 'I'm very sorry.' He looked over at P. P. Fan. P. P. Fan shook his head in disgust and turned to take his money out of the money sack. 'I'll try to do better next time.'

There was a long silence, then O'Yee said, 'Do you mean if it hadn't been for Yan you would have let the place be robbed?'

Spencer said, 'I'll get them next time. Honest.'

O'Yee said thoughtfully, 'Yan's been doing pretty well lately all things considered. He gave us that tip about the rope around the skeleton's ankles as well. He's turning into a pretty good—'

Spencer said, 'I came up with that!'

'With what?'

'The thing about the rope around the ankles! That was from me! I told Yan to pass it on to Feiffer. It was *my* idea.' He said, 'I told Yan he could have the credit, but—'

'He took it.' O'Yee said, 'Do you want to make a complaint about it?'

Spencer glanced at P. P. Fan. P. P. Fan did not glance at Spencer. 'No.'

There was a pause at the other end of the line then O'Yee said, 'Listen, Bill, let me give you a piece of advice: don't give things away until you're in a position where you won't notice losing them.' He said, 'You know, wait until you're in a position of power before you try to start doing good for everyone else. Wait until you're a Superintendent or something.'

Spencer said miserably, 'As opposed to a dumb copper.'

'Exactly.' O'Yee said consolingly, 'You'll get there one of these days. So why not wait until then?'

P. P. Fan looked at Spencer. P. P. Fan said unhappily, 'You're staying on?'

Spencer nodded.

O'Yee said, 'Do you see what I mean?'

'I'll hang on in case the real gang turn up.'

'Fine.'

Spencer said unhappily, 'I'm just a parish priest.'

O'Yee said, 'Pardon?'

'Priests have to wait until they're Popes to be able to dispense good.' He said, 'Like policemen.' He said, 'You just have to wait until you're powerful.'

O'Yee said, 'Oh.' He said, 'Well, anyway, think about it.' He said suddenly, 'Phew! I'll have to go.' He said again, 'Phew!' There was a radiator-shoving noise. He hung up.

Spencer said cheeringly to P. P. Fan, 'Well, that's one down.'

P. P. Fan said, 'Huh.'

47

Spencer said, 'Well, um—' He said, on a sudden brainwave, 'You're quite right about being powerful. My Senior Inspector was just saying the same thing.' He said in an orgy of flattery, 'You're quite right. Yes. Quite right. Of course you are. I'm just going to have to wait until I'm powerful.' He said, 'Yes . . . that's what I'm going to do . . . Absolutely right.' He said, to the bland face of P. P. Fan, 'Of course you are.' He opened the door to the storeroom and stepped in. He said, 'Right.'

P. P. Fan said bitterly, 'Hmmm.' He called out to the closed storeroom door, 'And just leave my valuable papers where they are!' He raised his voice and shouted at the door, the gods, the precepts of wisdom, and the virtuous acts of an experienced man rent asunder by the callousness of flaming youth, 'Just forget I ever told you anything!'

It was the last time he was ever going to fall for the old Merit in Heaven bit.

He went to count his dependable money.

The bell on the floorlight panel went *ding*! on the fourth floor to signal Round Two in the grudge match between Auden and the Oriental Elevator.

Auden said to the elevator, 'I'm getting out now. I'm going to let you go up and down and up and bloody down on your own for a while. I'm going down to the third floor on the stairs.' (He thought, "Good old stairs.") 'And I'm going to see just why you don't open on the third floor.' He said to the elevator, setting the rules of the match straight in its pulleyed mind, 'All right? And then I'm going to get into you again on the fourth floor and I'm going to work out just how you mug people on a floor you don't even serve.' He said ominously, 'Don't you think I won't.' He got out and watched until the doors closed and the elevator went on up.

He went towards the stairs.

It was cold in the storeroom: dark and dank, like a dungeon in the Tower of London or the Bastille, one of the smallest, worst, most inhuman and barbarous cells in the Château

48

D'If—a backroom in the New York Tombs, shut away in darkness and mould and desperation while the rest of the city was out skating on the rink at Rockefeller Plaza or walking in the sun in Central Park with children on the one day of the year the muggers took a holiday. The storeroom was the smelliest, most airless, cramped corner in the Black Hole of Calcutta—the boiler room of the Titanic after the boilers had shut down and bits of iceberg were sticking in through the plates. It was the corridor of Dracula's castle in Transylvania when the moon was hidden by clouds and all the doors were locked. It was Limbo. It was Purgatory. It was dreadful, evil, penitential. It was all those things, and more.

Spencer was happy.

He peered out into the main area of P. P. Fan's money-changing shop with the firm and unyielding conviction that if anyone deserved all those things in a small room, he did.

There was a tiny gadget just below the flaming core of the radiator's wick. If you could just reach it with a pencil and push it down, maybe it was possible to just...

O'Yee's pencil caught fire. He withdrew it sharply and stamped on it.

Right then, maybe if you got something like a screwdriver with a wooden handle you could keep it out of range until you just gave it a little push and...

He didn't have one.

The phone rang. O'Yee got up from his knees in front of the altar of the radiator and answered it.

An English voice said snappily, 'Who is this please?'

'Senior Detective Inspector O'Yee.'

There was a metallic crash somewhere behind the speaker. It sounded like someone dropping a surgical tray full of freshly sterilised instruments. The speaker said to the dropper, 'Get out!' then to O'Yee, 'Is Detective Chief Inspector Feiffer there?'

'No. Who's calling?'

There was yet another crash as the surgical tray dropper

compounded the dropping of the surgical tray by, on the way out, presumably dropping another. The voice said irritably, 'What's his first name?'

'Mr Feiffer's?'

'Yes.'

O'Yee said, 'Harry. Why? Who is this?'

'This is Dawson Baume calling from the Mortuary. Is he doing anything about that skeleton business?' There was yet another, but smaller, crash.

'He's out on it at the moment.'

'Ah.'

O'Yee waited.

'Ah.' The voice said to O'Yee, 'He's out on it now?'

'Yes.'

'Ah. "Harry," you said?'

'Yes.'

The voice said, 'Oh, good.' The voice said pleasantly, 'No need to tell him I called.'

5

The Organising Secretary of the Hong Bay Branch of the Vegetable Growers' and Market Gardeners' Association was a balding, fifty year old Chinese named, anonymously enough, Mr Lee. Mr Lee's office was on the third floor of the Association's building in Tiger Snake Road, accessible only by a narrow staircase that had an additional landing built on to it where none seemed structurally necessary halfway between the second and top floors. There was a shelf set into the chipped masonry wall by the landing and a piece of four-by-four wood bolted onto the banister that reminded Feiffer as he climbed the stairs of a gun platform. If it was, the gun had been taken away. He knocked on the thick oak door to Mr Lee's office and went in.

Mr Lee, sitting behind a heavy mahogany desk with his back to the corner of the wall, nodded. There were two little carved faces on the desk that looked like the sort of thing James Bond might have had on his Aston-Martin that could be converted into twin machine gun ports. Feiffer closed the door. It made a ringing metallic sound. Mr Lee said in English, 'Chief Inspector Feiffer.'

Feiffer nodded. He said, glancing back at the seven locks on the metallic door and the rear window to one side of the desk that evidently opened up onto an escape route across the roofs, 'You're Mr Lee.'

Mr Lee nodded.

'I assume the man on the front desk told you that I had an enquiry?'

Mr Lee nodded again. There was a circular discolouration on his right cheek that looked like a burn mark. Mr Lee turned that side of his face to him. Mr Lee said, still in English, 'I imagine most people say to you that they have no idea why the police would want to talk to them about anything—'

Feiffer started to say—

Mr Lee said acidly, 'Every day that the police do *not* want to talk to me about something, I'm surprised.' He touched the burn with his short fingers, 'I am of the firm conviction that the police in this Colony are the tools of the financial establishment and like nothing better than to persecute innocent people.' He said firmly, 'Whatever you want, however trivial or unimportant, I regret to say I know nothing about it.'

Feiffer glanced at a chair opposite the desk, 'May I sit down?'

'If you want to, you will.' Mr Lee said, 'Go ahead, pretend you take the possibility of my refusing seriously.' He said with heavy sarcasm, 'Please, oh please, be seated.'

Feiffer sat. He said pleasantly, 'I'd like some information about one of your members.'

Mr Lee touched the burn. He smiled. 'Which member is that? Sorry, never heard of him.'

'The one who grows sweet potatoes here in Hong Bay. He has a farm somewhere on the waterfront near Hop Pei Cove.'

'No one grows sweet potatoes as a cash crop on Hong Kong. They're all grown in the New Territories.' He said, beginning to rise, 'Well, that's sorted out. So sorry you can't stay—'

Feiffer said, 'Sit down!'

Mr Lee sat. He smiled. He reached for a thin box of cigarettes on the desk and took one out and lit it with a brass lighter. He looked up at Feiffer and indicated him with the cigarette. He asked evenly, 'I see you're wondering about the mark on my face? Do you want to know where I got it and what it is?' He said without waiting for an answer, 'It's a burn mark. From a petrol bomb. I got it here in Hong Kong during the 1966 riots.' He said, 'I have no love for running dogs of the capitalists.' He said, to make it clear, 'By which, I mean the police.'

'Since the riots in 1966 distilled down to a confrontation between the Communists and the police and the police armouries don't carry an issue stock of petrol bombs, I'm rather surprised you don't hold the Communists responsible.' Feiffer asked, 'Or is that too running-doggish?'

'It is totally beside the point who may have thrown the bomb, what counts is the reason for its being thrown in the first place.' Mr Lee said, 'The police, as usual, stood for the status quo. They, as usual, ignored totally the wishes of the masses who were demonstrating for their rights and freedom. The police—'

'Maybe the police were too busy protecting the rights of people that the demonstrators intent on *their* rights, forgot to take into account.' Feiffer said, 'There were a lot of people hurt. A large number of policemen included.'

Mr Lee said, 'There are casualties in every confrontation.'

'You appear to have been one of them.'

Mr Lee said, 'I'm not telling you anything about growers because I don't know anything.'

'I should remind you that withholding information—'

'I don't have any information. So I'm not withholding it.'

'The information I require concerns one of the members of the Association you represent.'

'In which case, my crime is that I am a very inefficient man. I should be more aware of my members and have a total mental file on each of them. But I do not. I confess to being stupid.' He pointed out evenly, 'In any event, since you haven't told me the name of the man you are looking for, I can hardly be expected to know—from my mental files—who he is.'

'I don't know his name.'

'I see. You merely want a list of people who grow a certain sort of crop.'

'Yes.'

Mr Lee nodded. 'In the same way the British wanted lists in Malaya when the Army of Liberation was operating. So that—'

'So I can locate someone specific.'

'So that in the event of more demonstrations of workers' solidarity for change the authorities will have a complete list of all food producers so they can burn or store the food to deny it to the true representatives of the masses.' He asked, 'As a matter of information, are you starting a rumour of impending trouble in order to justify further repression against the Chinese in the Colony?'

'As a matter of information, no.' Feiffer said, 'As a matter of information I am attempting to discover who it was disinterred a dead body and set it adrift on a raft.'

Mr Lee sighed a long sigh. 'Tell me why it is that the police, when it comes to crimes committed against Europeans are very ardent and, when committed against Chinese—' He said, 'You know, the Chinks: the lesser breeds—why they are less than ardent?' He said, 'There have been, for example, a series of muggings against Chinese in a certain apartment block in Hanford Road with no Europeans involved.' He said, 'Tell me why you are here asking questions about sweet potatoes on the strength of a highly unlikely story about corpses when you should be there.'

Feiffer said, 'There is a man there at the moment.'

'Who has discovered the identity of the mugger and arrested him?'

'Who is attempting to do so.'

Mr Lee nodded. 'A rather strange business to do with elevators that open on floors on which they do not open. Am I right?'

'Something like that.'

'You don't seem very certain.'

'I don't happen to wish to discuss it.'

'Oh.'

Feiffer said, 'I would have thought that since the people

who have been mugged have all been well-off you would have looked on their being robbed as rather a good job.'

'Some of them—one at least—is a good Socialist. His wealth has come from hard work.' Mr Lee said, 'In any event, none of them is that well-off.' He said, 'As a matter of fact, I have a cousin who lives there.'

'Then your cousin will tell you that something is being done.'

'Exactly what?'

'Why not ask your cousin?'

'I am asking you.'

'And I am not going to tell you.' Feiffer said, 'The man I am interested in talking to in relation to the disinterment has a farm on the waterfront and grows sweet potatoes.' He asked, 'Could you possibly rack your brain and tell me who it might be?'

'Why should it be one of my people?'

'Because the corpse was found with a rope around its ankles and a spirit-appeasement offering of sweet potatoes. I'm told that the rope-tying trick is a peasant superstition. And peasants with sweet potatoes to throw around are usually the ones who grow them.'

Mr Lee said, 'And because they are so superstitious and un-sophisticated they need a great deal of protection from the people who represent them. People like me.' He asked, 'When do you expect an arrest in the apartment muggings?' Mr Lee went on without pausing, 'I don't like you, Mr Feiffer, and I don't believe a word you say.' He said urbanely, 'It's due to my early training and also to my experience of life. I don't believe you people bother to do anything about the needs of ordinary Chinese and I don't believe you want to. I don't believe your story about dead bodies and sweet potatoes and I don't believe you're doing anything about the apartment muggings. I don't believe you've got a man there and if you have he's probably the one you can most spare who hasn't a hope in heaven of solving it. And I know you don't like me, so why the hell don't you just bugger off and go ask the Hong

Bay market gardeners who grows sweet potatoes and disinters skeletons?'

'Because without your say-so they won't tell me anything.'

'Right! Because I'm their elected—'

'Because you control the wholesalers and anyone who talks doesn't get to sell his crops—'

Mr Lee said, 'What a bad man I am. When all I'm trying to do is protect people. You go and protect people and maybe I'll help you.' He asked, 'What skeleton? What sweet potatoes?' He demanded significantly, 'What mugger? The mugger is real.'

Feiffer paused for a moment. He said slowly, 'I see. Some of your people—your cousin included—live in those apartments and they're complaining to you. Correct?'

Mr Lee did not reply.

'And you find you can't do anything—'

'I am doing something. I'm talking to you. I'm complaining about it. I'm trying to get information from you.'

'With as little success as I'm having from you.' Feiffer said, 'And you don't intend to tell me anything without getting something back in return. Am I right? You might consider lowering yourself to help the fascist cops—at great personal sacrifice and loss of face—but only if, in return, they promise to do something for you. Like getting the mugger. Well, all credit to you. Is that about the situation?'

Mr Lee smiled. He leaned back a little in his chair and glanced down at something behind his desk. (The buttons for the twin machine guns?) 'But you haven't *got* the mugger, have you?'

'We will.'

'Then—' Mr Lee leaned forward and tapped his cigarette carefully above a glass ashtray. '—no doubt at that time, miraculously it might seem to you, you will learn the identity of the farmer who grows sweet potatoes as a cash crop in Hong Bay.'

'There is only one?'

'There is only one.' Mr Lee smiled again, 'But for you to

56

find him unaided, Mr Feiffer, would be as difficult as it would be for, as they say, a dagger to go through the eye of a pig.'

'That's a camel to go through the eye of a needle.'

'Is it?' Mr Lee said coldly, 'Don't be too sure.'

The elevator doors on the third floor had been nailed shut. There were two three inch thick beams screwed across them and cemented into the brickwork on either side. Auden tested them. They were in there forever. He pressed his foot against the doors and pushed hard on them. They did not budge. He tested the beams again. Solid. He examined the screws. They were counter sunk into the wood and then locked into place by some sort of clear industrial adhesive. He put his fingernail against one of them to make sure it was a real screw head. It was a real screw head. He grasped the beams in both hands and pulled down on them to make sure they weren't just cleverly hinged. They weren't. They were cemented into the brickwork. He examined the door and the beams and the screws and the adhesive for signs of scratches or marks where someone had tampered with them. No one had. He looked at the wood of the beams themselves in case it was balsa. It was oak. He examined the elevator doors behind the beams. The doors were solid, re-inforced metal. "Hmm . . ."

He moved the call button at the side of the doors. The plate had been removed and where there had been the call mechanism there was now only a cavity. Even the cut leads from the mechanism had been removed and the holes cemented in. He looked at the floor indicator above the doors. The panel was covered with a rectangle of security wire, screwed in at each corner and plugged with the same clear adhesive.

He thought, "Anyone who could get those doors open is a bloody magician!"

He ran his hand along the wall on either side of the sealed doors looking for secret cavities. There were none. There was a payphone to one side of the wall. He tried to yank it free. It was fast.

There was a concrete flowerpot on the other side, evidently kept up by a resident from one of the apartments. Auden lifted it up to see what might be hidden under it. Cement floor and dirt. He put it back. He looked along the corridor facing the elevator and at the receding rows of doors to the third floor apartments. They were all the same. The first apartment facing the lift had two small windows at the side, but they were the only dissimilarity. Both the windows were curtained. Auden stamped on the floor of the landing to see if there was a secret trapdoor under it. There wasn't any secret trapdoor. He glanced at the lift doors again and then up at the lighted floorpanel. It showed the elevator was on the fourth floor, coming down.

He waited.

The elevator drew level with the third floor—he heard it stop behind the doors—and then went *click, click, click*! as it tried and failed to open the nailed, beamed, screwed and glued-up doors.

Auden rubbed his face. He watched the lights on the panel change to the second floor and then pause on the ground before the elevator started its journey up again. There was no one around on the third floor.

Auden said to the payphone, 'So how is it done?' He asked the potted plant, 'And what is it that always distracts the victim just before the door opens?' He thought, "If it wasn't for that distraction the victims would have seen the mugger waiting for them." He glanced at the doors and went over to test them again. They were sealed tight as the Sphinx.

He thought, "The mugger had to have been standing where I am so the panel lights could tell him that the elevator was coming down from the upper floors where the rich buggers live." He said to the beams, 'Then why is it no one's ever seen him doing it?' He said to the curtained windows of the elevator-facing apartment, 'And why have none of the victims seen him? What is it that distracts them just as the doors open on a floor on which the doors don't open?' He said to the potted plant, 'If I knew three or four people had been mugged on the third floor and the third floor doors opened on me, I wouldn't let myself be distracted by anything short of an atomic bomb!' He thought, "But they were and it was something so inconsequential and ordinary that they can't even remember what it was."

He said aloud, 'So how the bloody hell is it done?' He said to the cement floor under which there was no hidden trapdoor, '*I* don't bloodywell know!!' He sighed, 'Back to the bloody elevator.' He said to the elevator as it clicked its ineffectual way to the third floor and then gave up to go on to the fourth, 'Lousy, rotten, stupid *sod*!'

Way behind on points, he went up to the fourth floor to meet the elevator for Round bloody Three.

Mr Lee steepled his fingers under his chin.
He smiled. He looked at Feiffer.
He waited.

There was a man standing near the elevator on the fourth floor alternating between watering his pot plants near the wall payphone and smoking his cigar. He looked up as Auden appeared at the top of the emergency stairs and came towards him. He looked back to his plants by the side of the elevator then down to the steadily burning cigar in his hand and decided on the cigar. He put his red plastic watering can down and took a thoughtful puff on the cigar. He said warningly to Auden in careful English, 'I not speak English.' He glanced down at his plants—four of them in four cement pots—and shrugged.

Auden said in Cantonese, 'Who are you?'

The man lowered his cigar and took up his watering can. It had a short length of hosepipe pushed over its spout. He pushed it further back to secure it. He said pleasantly, 'Ong the Gardener. Unless you're trying to find someone.' He lifted up his cigar, 'In which case, I'm Ong the Cigar-Smoker.' He said, 'Ong the Gardener is a very ignorant fellow: the Cigar-

Smoker, on the other hand, like all cigar smokers, is slow, thoughtful and a man of opinions.'

Auden said, 'Huh.'

'Or, if it's something to do with the apartments, I'm Ong the Fourth Floor Resident. Gossip by the bucketload.' He said happily, 'Ong the Gardener for information about gardens, Ong the resident for gossip about the apartments and Ong the Cigar-Smoker for careful, thoughtful opinions.' He said, 'Speaking of which, who the hell are you anyway?'

Auden said, 'Auden the Cop.'

Ong said, 'Oh.' He picked up his can and went back to the watering. He told the plants, 'I suppose you're here about the muggings. I haven't the faintest and anyway it's all on the third floor, isn't it?' He said, smiling, 'It's all a bit too much for poor Ong.' He said to the cigar, 'Ong the Subservient Lesser Mind. If I were you I'd go and roust the people on the third floor, not the fourth. Ong the Snob is only too pleased to point out to you that people on the fourth floor won't have anything to do with those on the third and those on the fifth won't have anything to do with us.' He said, 'It's the way of the world and unless you happen to be a resident on the second or third floors the fact that the third floor is the abode of criminals surprises no one.' He said, 'Well, Ong the Punctual is now going back to his apartment to get on with some work.'

'Which apartment is that?'

'The one facing you.' Ong indicated the first flat facing the elevator. He took up his watering can, considered his cigar, and, Ong the Easily Bored Talking to European Cops went back to his apartment and closed the door.

The row of lights on the panel above the elevator doors went *ding*! for the second floor and the doors opened to no one. They shut again. Auden nodded to himself. Bloody typical. He thought, "The place is full of bloody lunatics." He thought, "The Old Empire just isn't what it used to be. In

60

the old Empire I could have had someone like Ong taken out and shot for insolence." He savoured the thought. He thought, "Nope, just not what they used to be. No respect for Sahibs." He thought, "When we had gunboats floating around up the Yangtse and down the Nile things were a bit different." He said hysterically to the rear wall of the elevator, 'A five-inch shell would sort *you* out for a bloody start!' He thought satisfactorily, "Whizz—boom! Rubble!"

The elevator went on down to the first floor, found no one waiting, and carried on down.

Auden thought, "The Chaps were different in those days. In those days you knew where you were. The White Man's Burden." He thought, "Good old Chaps. Foursquare old Rudyard Kipling." He considered it for a moment. "I'm the sort of Chap the Chaps would have liked. Burma, or the Sudan, or somewhere. People don't appreciate people like me anymore." The elevator doors opened and he thought, "I wouldn't have let the Empire fall to pieces. Not me." He thought, "Churchill wouldn't have let the Empire fall. And neither would I." The elevator doors opened onto the ground floor. Auden thought, "Good old Churchill—"

At his desk on the ground floor, the doorman glanced across to the elevator doors. The doorman was an enormous Indian ex-Subadhar-Major with a black patch over one eye, three rows of medals on his chest and a twelve gauge shotgun in a cradle under his desk. The doorman snapped to attention and shouted across the empty mezzanine, 'Sah!!'

Auden squared his shoulders and came out of the elevator at a dignified pace. He thought, "This is a bit more like it." He thought, "I'd forgotten about him." He said in his best officer-class drawl, 'Subadhar-Major...'

The Subadhar-Major shouted back, 'Sah!'

Auden noticed that one of the medals commemorated Indian independence. Well, you couldn't have everything. He inspected the Subadhar-Major casually. 'Nice turn out, Subadhar-Major.'

The Subadhar-Major couldn't possibly have been a day

61

under seventy. He looked, like most seventy-year-old men, as though he could run twenty-five miles before breakfast and then do two hundred push-ups to settle his digestion before moving onto the strenuous work of the day. Best to take the right line with the Locals straight away. They respected you for it. Auden shouted at the Subadhar-Major, 'Siddown!!'

The Subadhar-Major sat. He looked at Auden with his one glittering black eye.

Auden ignored the eye. The best way to deal with Native Dumb Insolence was to ignore it. Any Chap could tell you that. Auden shouted at the Subadhar-Major, 'Right! Just how many unauthorised people do you let into these apartments anyway? I know you're behind all this so you better just own up!' He demanded, 'Aye? Well? Speak up, man!'

There was a long pause. Then the Subadhar-Major began to swell. The Subadhar-Major said, 'WHAT?!'

'You heard me!' God, he was a big one! Auden said, 'Come on, out with it, damn you!' No lip from the Natives—straight to the point, devious buggers they were—a firm command from a White Man set their teeth chattering and reduced them to—

The Subadhar-Major crashed out, 'WHAT DID YOU SAY?'

Auden wavered. Mustn't waver. He wavered. Queen Victoria wouldn't have wavered. Auden wavered. The Subadhar-Major fixed him with his Eye. The Eye flashed at him and bored right through him. The Subadhar-Major rose to his feet and towered over him. The Subadhar-Major said, 'I'm going to assume I didn't hear you speak to me like that.' The Eye stared at him. The Subadhar-Major said, 'You ranting man, you!' That Eye in the grand old days of the Raj had sent young English subalterns into the billiards room with their Empire-issue Service Revolver loaded with one bullet at the rate on average of one a week. The Subadhar-Major said, 'What exactly do you think you are accusing me of in that loud and shouting tone?' He said in a voice that in the Khyber Pass had turned strong men to jelly, 'WELL?'

Auden said, 'If you don't let outsiders in to mug people then how is it done?'

The Subadhar-Major said, 'It's done by someone who lives here!' The Eye flashed.

Auden said, 'If it's someone who lives here how does he know when people are coming down from the top floors?' He said, 'Aye? Tell me that.'

'Because he watches the lights above the elevator! *I suppose!*'

'*You* watch the lights above the elevator!'

'*I* don't happen to be on the third floor!'

Auden shouted back, 'Neither is he!'

'Then he's somewhere else, isn't he!'

'Precisely! And he leans in and slugs them.' Auden said, 'And it could be you!'

'Could it?'

'Yes, it could!'

The Eye considered him. The Eye seemed to go blacker and more glittering. The Eye looked him up and down. The mouth below the Eye said very slowly and significantly, 'If *I* was going to slug someone in an elevator they wouldn't get up on the ground floor to tell someone.' The Eye said significantly, 'They'd be dead.' The Eye said slowly, 'And since the person who has found every victim so far on the ground floor has been me, maybe you could tell me how I manage to run down three floors faster than the elevator carrying the person I've slugged.' The Eye said, 'Well?'

'You tell me!'

The Subadhar-Major leaned back on his heels. If there was one thing that had always sorted out the Chaff Chaps from the Wheat in India it had been this one. The Subadhar-Major pursed his lips, 'No, sir, you tell me.' He said very pleasantly, 'You're the officer, not me.'

Auden wavered. Auden said, 'Well, I admit that the chances of—I admit that it's a pretty slim possibility that . . .' He glanced at the Eye, 'Since you put it that way . . .' Auden said quickly, 'You realise of course that I was only trying out one or two theories on you? You know, working on the assumption that if I pretended to be angry you might have come up with a spontaneous idea that so far you hadn't remembered . . .' He said, 'You know, for example, that, um . . .'

The Subadhar-Major nodded. He said politely, 'May I now be permitted to resume my humble duties?'

Auden said—He nodded. He shrugged. He shrugged again. 'Well . . .' Auden said, 'Well, back to the old elevator . . . aye?' He said quickly, 'Of course, a man of your background and record—' He said happily, 'Well, of course, you can see that it was just a strategy and that . . .'

The Subadhar-Major nodded.

'You can?' Auden said, 'Oh good.' He said again, 'Well, back to the old elevator for me . . . see you later perhaps? Aye.' He turned to go.

The Subadhar-Major said very softly, 'Sah . . .' He shook his head. He fingered his Indian independence medal.

Auden said Chappishly, 'Well . . .' He said, 'Well, *jolly good!*'

He went back to the elevator, waited until the doors had closed on the ground floor, and then, glancing up at the ceiling of the elevator, the call buttons, the floor panel that lit up and went *ding*! the emergency telephone, the stupid sign about four children and two adults and no children or no children and no adults, he turned to the rear wall of the elevator and, aiming carefully, for the next three floors, did his best to kick it to bits.

In the Detectives' Room, a sluggish brown cat appeared at the half open door and dragged itself languidly past the radiator, clumped heavily up onto a shelf of files and manoeuvered itself behind them to find somewhere to sleep. It reminded O'Yee of Auden. He glanced at his watch and calculated that if Auden, like the cat, hadn't found somewhere to sleep, he would have been riding up and down over in the Cathay Gardens apartments for almost six hours.

64

O'Yee had a call booked to the Records Clerk of the American Embassy for when the clerk came back from lunch.

He thought he had better do something about Auden while he still thought of it.

6

Mr Lee picked up his phone at the first ring, listened for a moment, and then handed the instrument over towards Feiffer. 'Cop talk.' He leaned back in his chair and glanced down at the controls of whatever armament some obliging carpenter cum gunsmith had fitted there for him at one time, 'Please forget I'm here. Carry on with your private conversation.' He said venomously, 'Ask him if he's got the Cathay Gardens mugger?'

'Feiffer.'

'Harry? Christopher.' O'Yee waited for a salutation.

There was no salutation. Feiffer's eyes stayed on Mr Lee. Feiffer said, 'What do you want? Has Auden come up with anything on the elevator job?'

Mr Lee muttered, 'Auden. Well, at least that's a more impressive invention than Smith or—'

O'Yee said, 'No, Auden hasn't come up with anything on the—'

'Then what do you want?'

Mr Lee mimicked, 'Auden? Who's Auden? What are you talking about?'

Feiffer said evenly, 'Auden is a Detective Inspector stationed at Yellowthread Street. Feel free to look it up in the Government Gazette.'

Mr Lee attempted to look chastised. He said softly, 'Bollocks.'

O'Yee said, 'What did you say?'

Mr Lee shook his head in contemplation at the triggers,

buttons, butts, ammunition carriers or whatever it was he could see built into his desk, 'What heading do I look under? Figments of the Police Imagination?'

'Go to hell.'

O'Yee said, hurt 'What did I say?'

'Not you.' Feiffer said irritably, 'What do you want? Is it about Auden or not?'

'Yes it's about Auden!' In the Detectives' Room, O'Yee looked over at the stack of files and folders behind which, safe from the vicissitudes of the world, the cat had taken refuge. 'Auden has been in that elevator for almost six hours without a break and I thought you, as the superior officer from whom all grace and goodness flows, might feel it was time to give the poor bastard a break!'

'Auden is to stay where he is.' Every time he said it, Feiffer thought the name sounded less and less like a real person. It sounded like he was saying it in inverted commas "Auden." (For "Auden" read Code Six: the top secret assault on . . .) Feiffer said, 'He's there to catch the mugger. The only way he's going to be able to do that is to be there. Is that clear?'

'Oh, yes! Pardon me for looking on him as a flesh and blood person! Or any of us! Hot damn, what a mistake! We're all little metal wind-up dolls! How could I forget that?' O'Yee did his impression of Robbie the Robot, 'The-metal-men-of-Planet-Zark-are-yours-to-command.'

'Have you been on to the American Embassy about—about our friend?'

'Yes, I've been on to the American Embassy about our friend. The American Embassy is going to ring back about our friend. When the American Embassy rings back about our friend I will ring you back about what the American Embassy said about our friend. I won't even stop to oil my cogs. For you, I'll work straight on until I rust!' The radiator lashed out a sunspot of fire and woke the cat. The cat peered out from behind a folder, decided the world was unworthy of its attention, and reversed back behind the folder again. If, as the Buddhists believed, it was the reincarnation of an earlier life, then whoever had had that earlier life had had his head screwed on when it came to picking reincarnations. 'Is there anything else or can I go back to holding the world up with my single untiring bicep?'

Mr Lee put his fingers together under his chin in an attitude of world-weariness and stared at the ceiling.

Feiffer said into the phone, 'Tell Auden I want a result.'

'So he's to stay on.'

'He's to stay there until he gets a result. And I want you to ring me back as soon as you hear from the Embassy.' There was silence from the other end of the line, 'Are you still there?'

O'Yee made a clicking sound with his teeth. 'This is a recording. Senior Inspector O'Yee—'

'And I can do without your attempts at levity.' He glanced at Mr Lee considering the mildew spots on the ceiling. 'The Cathay Gardens job is important. To some extent, the other job hangs on it—unless you'd care to spend the rest of your life poking around the farming community of Hong Bay discussing the weather and the sweet potato crop.' He was about to add, 'Look, Christopher, the reason I'm so jumpy about all this is . . .' but one glance at Mr Lee's face dispelled that thought, 'So just get on with it, will you? And why the hell is the Embassy ringing back? Don't they have any staff?'

'Their staff is on lunch.' O'Yee said testily, 'Hard to credit, isn't it? My God, what a thought: there are actually a few far-flung countries left in the world where the workers actually get lunch.' He said loudly before Feiffer could say anything, 'But I'll get onto them again now. I'll shout at them and abuse them and kick the shit out of them and tell them who I'm ringing for: Feiffer the Cur of the East—by God, I'll talk some sense into those soft-bellied food-eating Yanks!' The radiator made a vicious roaring noise and he shouted at it across the room, 'And you can shut up too! And apart from anything else, I want to ask the Embassy for something on my own behalf—something solely, completely, strictly and uniquely for myself! O.K?'

There was silence from Feiffer's end of the line.

O'Yee demanded, 'Ask me what!'

'All right. What do you want to ask them for?'

'Bloody political asylum!' There was a momentary pause and then at his end of the line, he slammed the phone down, hard.

Mr Lee said sweetly, 'Any luck, Chief Inspector?'

Maliciously, he smiled.

Inside the moving elevator Auden glanced up at the floor panel above the doors. The elevator was moving down from the sixth floor to the fifth. He watched the light go out for the sixth and flick on for the fifth. There was a *ding!* as the mechanism signalled the fifth floor.

There was a *ding!* Auden glanced backwards. The telephone went *ding!* as the elevator doors opened for the fourth floor, caught, and then began ringing full stride. Auden picked it up from the cradle and said, 'Auden.' He glanced back at the panel casually. The light on the panel read 5. He thought, "That's odd." He glanced out at the number painted on the opposite wall on the floor. It also read 5. He thought, "That's strange, I thought it should have been 4." He said into the phone, 'Who is this?'

He stopped. He thought—

He said aloud to himself, 'It couldn't be that—'

He said in an awestruck voice, 'It is!' He said into the phone, 'My God, it is!' He said for the third time, *'My God, it bloody is!'*

Mr Lee handed Feiffer the telephone with a look of long-suffering on his face, glanced significantly skywards and then down at a sheaf of papers on his desk. There was a poster in Chinese pinned to a notice board on one wall of his office exhorting the masses to solidarity with the struggle of the Chinese peasants to increase their cauliflower yield in Szechuan province and that too he gazed at with meaning. Feiffer's snub-nose revolver was visible in its leather holster for a moment as he leant forward to take the phone. Mr Lee looked back at the poster and shook his head.

O'Yee's voice on the other end of the line said meekly, 'Well, it's me again.' He hurried on before the abuse could start, 'You asked me to get a result from Auden. Well, I rang him and he thinks he's got a result.' He said in an encouraging tone, 'Isn't that good news?'

'Has he made an arrest?' Feiffer's eyes travelled to Mr Lee. Mr Lee looked surprised. He waited, listening. Feiffer said theatrically, 'So Auden's made an arrest, has he? Well, well. Good work.' He smiled maliciously at Mr Lee.

Mr Lee said, in spite of himself, 'Has he?'

O'Yee said, 'No.'

'I thought you just said he'd—' (Mr Lee leaned back, smiled again, and looked confirmed.)

'No, I said he's got a *result*. He thinks he knows how it's done. How the elevator opens at a floor it's not supposed to open at. He's hanging on now to see if he can check it. He wouldn't say what his theory was, but I got the impression he's sure he's right. How are your bones coming along? Any information from Lee the friend of the struggling masses?'

'Not a lot, no.'

'Is there anything I can do from this end?'

'You can tell me what the Embassy had to say.'

'They haven't said anything. Harry, it's only been about ten minutes since I spoke to you before. They're still out on lunch. They said someone would ring as soon as possible.'

'Can you hurry them up?'

'Pardon?'

'I said, can you hurry them up?'

There was a momentary silence. When he spoke, O'Yee's San Francisco accent sounded very strong. O'Yee said, shocked, 'You don't ring up the Embassy of the United States of America and hurry them up! The Embassy of the United States of America hurries you up! Do you know how many people there are just queuing up at the Visa desk of your average U.S. Embassy every hour of the day?' O'Yee said in tones of mock incredulity, 'Good Heavens! And apart from that I went through that whole routine with them the first time I rang. You obviously have no idea what a popular place the U.S. of A. is to be these days.'

'I'm surprised anyone would want to leave it in the first place.'

There was a pause. 'They should get back to me in about twenty minutes. Will you still be with Lee?'

'Probably.'

'Then I'll ring you there.'

Feiffer paused. He looked over at Lee, listening and began, 'Listen, Christopher, about my tone earlier—' but O'Yee at the other end, in the pause, had hung up.

In the storeroom of P. P. Fan's, Spencer was taking stock of his miserable existence. He had the Winchester in his hand and as he totted up the ledger columns of his failure he loaded it and twisted at it and undid bits and pieces of its construction obsessionally. He slid his fingers into the loading port at the bottom of the receiver, pressed the cartridge retainer and slid out one of the rounds. It flipped out onto his palm. He thought: "I was given a chance to learn something about commerce and I threw it away." He withdrew the second cartridge: "My attitude was all wrong." The third round: "I should have seized the opportunity with both hands and paid it back by being vigilant." He thought, "And I didn't. I let myself down." He reached up and undid the gas valve retaining nut on the forestock. "I gave all the credit to Yan for that thing about skeletons and ghosts because I thought I'd get so much more credit from being a tycoon it wouldn't count." The retaining nut came off and he pulled the barrel assembly forward and separated the wooden forestock from it: "I was so busy feeling clever, Yan had to come in and do my job for me." Then the barrel came away cleanly from the receiver and he pushed a seating pin in the frame and removed the entire trigger plate and mechanism, "I'm a failure." He put all the bits on the floor. The gun, in the gloom, looked like an ad for an exploding Winchester shotgun, "Thank God, at least Constable Yan was on the ball." He flicked out the aerial of the walkie-talkie to call him.

There was no reply. Obviously, having done his job, he had gone away in disgust. Spencer thought, "I'm a pariah."

There were cobwebs in the roof-corners of the room, but even the spiders seemed to have deserted. Spencer thought, "I'm just going to have to stay here forever." In Westerns, when the cowardly gunfighter moved to a backwater of civilisation there was always an obliging Broderick Crawford character who would turn up in the last reel to be shot dead by the coward, and a girl, who believed in the coward, to believe in him even more when he was a hero. In *The Fastest Gun Alive*, the townspeople had pretended to bury Glenn Ford after he had shot Broderick Crawford to keep him safe from fast-draw artists now that he had proved himself a man. Spencer thought that with Bill Spencer in the same position the townspeople would have paid for emergency surgery on the dying Broderick Crawford so that the dying Broderick Crawford could flicker back to life and shoot Bill Spencer dead.

There was a broken pair of half spectacles on the floor of the storeroom together with an old cardigan with holes in the elbows (obviously the artifacts of an aged clerk who had finally given up the ghost) and Spencer wondered whether it was possible to cut one's own throat with optical lenses or smother oneself to death on a sleeve.

He tried the walkie-talkie again. It was silent. P. P. Fan's voice called out, 'You! Don't touch anything in there!' and Spencer replaced the broken spectacles and the holey cardigan on the floor and hung his head.

In his shop, behind his counter, staring fixedly at the storeroom door, P. P. Fan was working himself up. He had a wad of mixed Singapore dollars and Thai bahts in his hand and twice, *twice* in the last five minutes he had lost count of them and had to start again at the beginning. His blood boiled. He stared at the closed storeroom door behind which sulked the nemesis of his life and shouted, 'You don't even know that the Arabic language the Arabs write down has a totally different vocabulary from the Arabic language the Arabs actually speak! You're the sort of idiot who, seeing the rise of the oil states and expecting to be able to cash in, learns the Arabic language they write down and trots along to have a chat to some Sheik about making money!' He tried to count the money again and made a mess of it, 'Why of all the people in the world, were *you* sent to plague me?' He thought he heard a whisper from the storeroom, 'It's no use now apologising— my sole hope is that somehow, sooner or later, this day will end! You want to see me in bankruptcy court!' He said to himself in a horrified tone of voice, 'I couldn't have died without knowing it, could I? This couldn't be my eternal punishment for my bad deeds?' His voice climbed again, 'What bad deeds? I tried to do good and look how you repaid me!'

Spencer opened the door a fraction. (Mr Fan shouted 'No! Don't come out here!') His foot scattered a few bits of the dismantled shotgun. 'I'm very sorry, Mr Fan . . .'

Mr Fan shrieked, 'Get away! Get back inside your room!'

Spencer hunched back from the door and pulled it closed with a gentle click.

Mr Fan yelled, 'You dumb—' He searched for the word, 'You dumb . . . *COP*!'

In Mr Lee's office, Feiffer waited. Mr Lee sat in sepulchral silence gazing at the poster on his wall. He glanced at the telephone on the desk and then to Feiffer. Feiffer thought of long dead white-bleached bones and a shape under a sheet on a bitterly cold steel tray that had once been a man. His eyes travelled to Mr Lee's cigarette in the ashtray. The cigarette had gone out. He thought of the silence in the mortuary room: long, eternal nothingness . . . Mr Lee said suddenly, 'I suppose any old scapegoat will do.' His voice came out cracked. He cleared his throat. He shrugged, 'I suppose your man Auden-or-whatever-his-name-is is going to decide some poor bastard looks stupid enough to confess to anything and then he's going to pull him in and take his commendation.' He sounded unsure of himself, 'I suppose that's what your man Auden's got planned, isn't it?'

Feiffer did not reply.

Mr Lee said, 'Sure. Any old scapegoat will do. Never mind the honest people who are going to go on being mugged. I suppose the theory is that if you pull in some poor idiot and put him away, the real mugger will get frightened and lay low for a while. I suppose that takes the pressure off you, doesn't it?' He touched the burn mark on his cheek, 'I know how you people work all right. I've had experience with you people before.' He squirmed forward in his chair uncomfortably, 'I don't know why I don't just assume the worst and tell you the name of your sweet potato farmer and have done with it!'

'Why don't you then?'

'I suppose because I live in hope that one day the police might actually do their job and protect the masses!' He said, 'The innocent hard-working people in those apartments and—'

'And your cousin—'

'That's got nothing to do with it!' Mr Lee asked abruptly, 'Percentage-wise, what are the chances of this man Auden actually catching the mugger?'

'Percentage-wise, I have no idea.'

'Is he good—this Auden?'

'He's competent, yes.'

Mr Lee touched his face again. He gazed ahead for a moment. 'No one's actually suggesting in the real world that the cops threw petrol bombs. You know that as well as I do—and don't you start to lean forward like that so you can be condescending and say, "Quite right, my dear fellow." All right?'

'Why are you getting so angry about it? I've told you what we're doing. You're the one who's being difficult.'

'And you're just going to hang about in my office until you break me down, is that it?'

'I thought we had a bargain. A *quid pro quo*. The mugger for the name of the farmer.'

Mr Lee said sullenly, 'Some miserable scapegoat.' He touched his face again. He said angrily, 'It's not up to me to go charging around finding muggers. What am I supposed to do—find him and beat him to death? We're a respectable Union, not a secret society—!'

'No one's asking you to go charging around beating people up.'

'But if you come up with the wrong man I'll have to, won't I? I'll have to get my thugs to go in and—' He said in parenthesis, 'If I had any thugs—well, it's just not on in my position, is it?' He demanded angrily, 'Can I offer you a cup of tea?'

'Pardon?'

'Well, if you're going to hang around here like some sort of legless ghost I might as well try and make things comfortable for you, mightn't I? For all I know, this Auden character might even get the right man.' He waved his hand angrily in the air, 'Forget it! Forget I offered you anything!'

'I'll take the tea.'

Mr Lee said suddenly, quietly, 'I've got a position to uphold.' He bunched his fist to emphasise the point, 'People expect things of me and I have to act in a certain—' He snapped, 'Do you want the tea or not?'

'I've already said so.'

Mr Lee said, 'Good.' He shouted out in the direction of the steel door at the top of his voice, '*TEA!*' He said vehemently, 'I hope it chokes you.'

Across the city, in the elevator of the Cathay Gardens bachelor apartments, Auden, smiling, contemplating in turn his gun, his handcuffs, and a steadily growing desire for bloody and total revenge, planned his strategy.

7

Auden came out of the elevator on the ground floor and staggered with the accumulated vertigo. The Subadhar-Major looked at him and made a sharp sniffing noise. The elevator doors closed and Auden turned around and looked at them, then watched the lights on the floor panel as the lift went automatically up to the seventh floor, halted at the point at which a key was needed to transport it up to the eighth, ninth and tenth floors, then, clicking, began travelling back down again. There was an odd wise smile on Auden's face. He nodded to himself and watched the flickering lights above the panel as they signalled the elevator's descent. He had a bunch of keys in his pocket and he jangled them in time to the flickering lights: flick-jangle-flick—then he made a cackling sound, turned on the Subadhar-Major and fixed him with a demented stare.

The Subadhar-Major had seen it all before: Indian-madness. Auden leaned forward and patted the elevator doors with his left hand, caressed it for a moment. He jangled his keys again. The Subadhar-Major started to come forward gently. First, you took the poor soul carefully under the arms and steered him towards the base hospital, then you helped the medics undress him from his sweat-stained battle dress, remove his ammunition boots (being very deft about getting his Service revolver away before the poor devil noticed it) and then puff! the unfortunate young lunatic was whisked off on a long sea-cruise back home to a quiet private hotel in Brighton full of spinsters and retired headmasters. The CO usually recommended a medal to go along in the man's kit and the War Office made him up a rank to see the pension was adequate. Standard procedure. The Subadhar-Major thought, "Poor bastard, he was just the type. I guessed it straight away." He reached Auden and extended his hand.

Auden spun on him.

The Subadhar-Major stepped back. You could never tell when one of these people might be dangerous.

Auden said, 'I've got it!'

The Subadhar-Major nodded.

'It was so simple, but it took a good brain to finally trigg to it!' Auden said with a wild gleam in his eye, 'I've been riding up and down, up and down, up and down in that frigging elevator for over six hours and I've finally got it!' The eyes gleamed brightly at the Indian, 'Not bad, aye?'

The Subadhar-Major said quietly, 'No, very good indeed. My word, yes, most excellent. Very good indeed, sir.' He tried to see Auden's gun and other deadly weapons so he could deftly remove them. They were not visible under his coat. He asked, 'Have you got a gun of any type, sir?'

Auden's eyes concentrated on the elevator doors as he polished the final edges of his plan. He extended a decisive finger at the Subadhar-Major, 'Now, after riding up and down and up and down in the elevator all morning, what I have to do now is . . .' He paused for a moment at the wonderful simplicity of it all, ' . . . *is walk up the stairs!*' He said to himself in anticipation of his triumph, 'Ah-ha!' He asked the Subadhar-Major, one servant of the Empire to another, 'You see it now, don't you? Of course! It's so bloody obvious!'

'Oh, yes, sir . . .' The Subadhar-Major steeled himself to get the great mitt firmly under Auden's arm.

Auden said, '*Right!*' He moved forward as the hock-hand came under-arming towards him, almost galloped to the door to the emergency stairs, paused for a moment, waved bravely and said, 'See you later.' He saw the Subadhar-Major off balance on the parquet floor, one hand out as if he were trying to catch someone, thought, "Poor bastard, he's getting on a bit," counselled, 'Mind your balance there, Subadhar-Major,' and started up the stairs.

On the landing of the seventh floor, he stopped. Through the thick masonry of the stairwell, he could hear the elevator travelling up and down in its tunnel. The steel door that led to the rich buggers' apartments on the upper three floors was locked. He paused for a moment, selected the right key from the master set he had brought with him, undid the lock, went up the stairs and stepped out onto the thick purple carpet of the eighth floor. He closed the door carefully behind him and walked quietly to the elevator.

He looked up to the floor panel above the elevator doors. The elevator was between the third and second floors, going down. Auden thought, "The old magic third floor that doesn't open." Now that he knew all, it seemed so childishly simple. He waited for exactly fourteen minutes, smoking a cigarette until the time was ripe, then hesitating for a moment like a Pentagon General savouring the thought of unleashing a cruise missile into the darkest depths of the Kremlin, inserted the key into the elevator call panel. He drew a breath . . . and then turned it. The lights on the floor panel hovered for a moment, going down. The electrical impulse registered: this was a signal from on high—one of the rich buggers demanding that the elevator serve him first. The elevator ceased hovering: it came directly up towards the eighth floor in, Auden supposed with vehement anthropomorphical loathing, an oily lather of servility. Auden watched it come up. It reached the eighth floor, there was a *ding*! and there, resplendently opening onto the opulence of the purple carpet, was the elevator.

Auden said evilly, 'Hullo, you bastard, I've worked out how you do it.' He stepped inside and paused for a moment with his hand holding the doors from closing. With his free hand, he put the keys back in his coat pocket and unclicked his handcuffs from the back of his belt. He let the doors go and they slid closed as he pressed the GROUND button.

Licensed to carry two adult persons or one adult and two

*children, or four children only. Unaccompanied children
are not permitted to travel in this elevator.*
(And the same below in Chinese characters.)
(Auden the all-knowing smiled benignly.)

He put his hand into the circlet of the doubled over hand-cuffs and tested their potential as knuckle-dusters. They seemed to have quite some potential. He found his spot—a little to one side of the doors on the right hand side—and looked up at the floor panel. If he was there, the mugger had seen the lift go empty to the eighth floor and had made two assumptions: *one* that it was going up to the eighth floor because one of the rich buggers was calling it, and *two*, that because it had gone up to the rich buggers' floor and was empty as it went up Auden, the-about-to-be-bane-of-his-life, little-did-he-know, had given up in disgust at his own stupidity and gone home. If the mugger was there.

Auden bunched his fist around the steel handcuffs and thought, *"Be there . . ."* The elevator opened and closed on the seventh floor.

The light on the floor panel changed to *6*. There was a *ding!* and the doors opened onto nothing and then closed again.

Auden waited. The doors closed again as the elevator moved downwards.

The lights on the panel went to *5*. There was a *ding!* The doors opened again.

Auden thought, "So far, so good . . ." He thought, "Not a soul around. There never is when the mugger does his job." The doors closed again and he looked up at the floor panel above the doors. The light was about to move down to *4*. He thought, "Here it comes . . ." He said softly to himself, 'Wait for it . . .' He drew back the handcuff-encased fist.

There was a *ding!* It was the telephone. He almost turned to look at it. He willed himself, "Telephone, telephone, don't look—" then there was an almost simultaneous *ding!* and the doors opened and the mugger, ski-masked, holding something long and hard in his hand reached in before the doors had

79

fully opened and went 'Thwack!' in a long swinging motion. The masked head came in in the same moment. The slit eyes in the mask stared for a split second, the thick woollen mask felt a thick hand wrench it forward and then, in the joyous culmination of six hours up and down, up and *fucking* down, Auden pole-axed him with the handcuffs.

Auden looked up at the floor light panel. It read *4*. Auden looked down at the groaning body on the floor of the elevator. He said in an evil tone, 'Funny. I thought it should have been *3*.' He said in a happy voice loaded to the gills with sarcasm, 'Oh, how strange, the telephone bell and then being almost hit over the head as the panel bell went off a second later confused me. I thought I was mugged on the third floor. Oh, how silly of me.' He reached down and stripped Ong's mask off and relieved him of the lead-filled watering can hosepipe. The elevator doors began to close, struck Ong's thighs half way out, and then opened again. Then they hit Ong on the thighs again and opened again. Ong said, 'Ooohh . . .' He turned painfully onto his shoulder and looked up at Auden. Then the doors hit him yet again.

Auden said formally, 'I arrest you for assault and battery on dates and times to be specified on the charge sheet. You are not obliged to say anything, but if you do say anything . . .' He thought, "By God, I'm enjoying this." 'Then I have to warn you that whatever you say may be taken down in writing and given in evidence.' He smiled at Ong as the doors hit him yet again and asked, 'Do you understand what I have just said to you?'

'Yes.' Ong reached up and felt his head. He said sadly, 'Ong the badly bruised.'

Auden grinned at him without an atom of sympathy. He said happily, 'Ong the Apprehended.'

Ong said, 'Ohhh.' He looked up with pain and disgrace in his eyes, 'Ong the Humiliated.' He made a sniffing sound, 'Ong the Soon to be Incarcerated. Ong the—'

Auden said, 'Shut up.' He slipped the handcuff-knuckle-dusters back carefully into his pocket, gazed around the elevator with the airy disinterest of a master to whom all the secrets of the universe are as dust on the palm of his hand and smiled benificently. He reached down and pulled Ong's legs into the elevator, thought for a glorious happy moment of the look on the Subadhar-Major's face when this little lot opened onto his ground floor, thought of his six hours up and down and up and bloody down, drew himself up to his full height and puffed out his chest and said very clearly and succinctly in English:

'Auden the fucking *Detective*!'

The elevator, that mere machine, obedient to his every whim, went down to the ground floor carrying its triumphant load of Holmes and Moriarty.

The phone rang. Feiffer took it from Mr Lee and listened for a moment. O'Yee's voice said, 'Harry?' He paused at the other end of the line. Feiffer's eyes moved to Mr Lee, watching him. 'Auden's got him.'

'The mugger?'

'Auden's got him in custody. They just came through the door. He's at the front desk being charged now.'

Feiffer repeated for Mr Lee's benefit, 'Auden's got the mugger and he's being charged now.'

'Right.' There was a pause as O'Yee shuffled some papers and a phew! as presumably, the radiator bathed him in a sudden heatwave, 'His name's Ong. One of the residents of the apartments. Apparently, he fixed the emergency telephone in the elevator so people thought it was a signal for the next floor. Then when he clobbered them on the fourth floor at almost the same moment as the second bell went off, they got confused and thought they were being clobbered on the third. Instead of being clobbered on the fourth. Simple, isn't it? Well, anyway, Auden says it's simple. I couldn't get a lot of sense out of him. I think the vertigo probably got to him. He kept mumbling something about someone having to call him "Sahib." ' He shuffled some more papers, 'Anyway, he's got him and that's the main thing. The American Embassy still hasn't called me back about the identification of the skeleton.'

'Ong. Right?'

'That's it. I haven't got a first name. I can go around to the desk and find out if you like.'

'No. Thanks very much. Stick with the Embassy.'

'Will you still be there?'

Feiffer looked at Mr Lee and put his hand over the mouth-piece, 'My Senior Inspector wants to know whether I'll still be here trying to get information out of you now that we've got the mugger, or whether I'll—'

Mr Lee shook his head. He opened his hands in studied resignation.

'I'll be here for about another three seconds. Then I'll be—'

Mr Lee said, 'You'll be on a sweet potato farm on the waterfront.' He glanced up at the poster and grimaced.

'I'll be in the car, Christopher.' He said again, 'Thanks very much.'

'Well, that's perfectly all right. We here at Mission Control —the unsung heroes of the small back rooms—we have no human desire except to serve. Our only delight is to—'

Feiffer said evenly, 'Good. In that case, delight me by getting onto the Embassy.' He hung up and looked expectantly at Mr Lee.

Mr Lee's eyes stayed on the poster. He said, 'The farmer's name is Kwok.'

Feiffer said, 'Good God, don't tell me you actually believe we've got the right man?'

'Nobody fails all the time.'

Feiffer said, 'Ong.'

'Yes.'

'One of your people?'

'No, he's not in my Union.'

'Oh? An acquaintance?' Feiffer asked innocently, 'Maybe a—'

'All right!' Mr Lee said, 'No one's accused you of being *stupid*! All I accused you of was being a tool of the capitalists —I didn't say you were actually *stupid*!' He said, 'I know you know—I'm not stupid either.' He paused for a moment, 'The farmer's name is Kwok. He's got Lot number 568 along the waterfront in Hop Pei Cove. All right?'

'All right.' Feiffer rose to go. He looked down at Mr Lee as Mr Lee's hand went to a control under his desk to unlock the armour-plated door.

Mr Lee said softly, 'This fellow, Ong.' He pressed the button and stood up as the door made a series of unlocking sounds. He paused for a moment, briefly toyed with the notion of putting out his hand in farewell, and thought better of it, 'He's my cousin.' (Feiffer said with heavy irony, 'You surprise me.') 'I always suspected it was him.' He said quickly, 'But you won't get anything out of Kwok. He doesn't know anything about anything.'

'He knows about something.'

'About skeletons? All he knows is that he dug it up and got so scared that it might bring him bad luck he put it on a home-made raft with a few good-fortune symbols and pushed it out into the South China Sea.' Mr Lee said victoriously, 'He came to me first thing and told me what he'd done.' He wore his victory without rancour: 'So, you see, I knew all along.' Mr Lee said grandly, 'I have a position to maintain. I'm very good at it.'

'So I've noticed.'

'I've covered myself nicely. I've protected my Union members from a terrible mugger and at the same time used the cops to rid my family and myself of a great potential embarrassment. Now Ong goes away for ten years, the farmers love me, Kwok has had the advantage of my defending him to you before you turn up to confuse him and, generally, I've come out of this looking pretty good.'

Feiffer said, 'And in Peking they think, "By Heaven, there's a man who knows how to swim in the river of repression and use it to his own ends." '

Mr Lee nodded.

Feiffer said, 'I envy you your brilliance.' He said evenly, 'And the main thing is that you kept your loyalties to the people uncompromised.' (Mr Lee nodded.) 'I mean, it wouldn't have done at all for you to be seen taking the side of a member of your family who went around mugging people. Would it?'

'Now, to be fair, Chief Inspector, he only mugged the rich.

'But terrified the poor, Mr Lee.'

'Agreed.' Mr Lee waved his hand dismissively, 'Well, anyway, I'm finished with him now.'

'God help you if it ever came out that you in some way supported a member of your family who was so politically uneducated he did the things Ong did.' Feiffer said, 'Holy proletariat, that wouldn't look good for you at all.'

Mr Lee said suspiciously, 'What are you getting at?'

'Nothing.' Feiffer extended his hand and Mr Lee took it grudgingly, 'I'll go and see your man Kwok. With many thanks.' He turned towards the door.

Mr Lee watched him go. There was something just a little too smug about . . . He wondered what Feiffer had . . . He stood at the desk for a long moment staring out the open door . . .

Mr Lee shouted suddenly at the top of his voice, 'Oh, no! That bastard Ong is going to come to me for *bail*!'

Everything in P. P. Fan's was quiet. Mr Fan finished counting his wad of notes and checked the pencilled-in total on the wrapper. It was correct. He took up a New Zealand ten-dollar note, a hundred Swiss franc note, a handful of coins in the various small denominations of Laos, Iran and Yugoslavia, two Tibetan Government promissory notes and a Tongan bank draft and converted them all into a single Hong Kong dollar gold exchange rate in his head and knew he was correct. He looked around for something harder. There were a few illegal Moroccan dirham in a box awaiting some unscrupulous traveller to Marrakech and he flicked his mind over and worked out a good rate on them first in U.S. currency, then Spanish pesetas, and then, just in case a Luxembourger came in, into Luxembourg francs allowing a slight discount for the trouble the Luxembourger would have to go to in Agadir or Ouarzazate to convince an illegal currency buyer that Luxembourg was a separate country and not just part of Belgium. The equation came out like the result from an IBM computer.

The old brilliance was back again. The idiot in the storeroom was either asleep or dead and, in the cathedral of his money-changer's brain, all was well. The old P. P. Fan, hardly having missed a single beat, was functioning again. The human economic forecaster was back at the old stand. P. P. Fan glanced casually out towards his front door to see who the lucky next recipient of a life's study of the perils and joys of money was going to be. He smiled to himself optimistically as, at the exact same moment, as if at a single soundless signal, the members of The Deaf and Dumb Gang watching from across the street, having at last concluded that his was the latest financial emporium worthy of their attention, decided to pay a call.

Something one of them carried under his coat made a clicking noise as he cocked it.

8

In the Mortuary, Dawson Baume slipped on his surgical rubber gloves and turned to look at the outline of the skeleton under the sheet. He pursed his lips for a moment and then glanced up at the tiled ceiling above the steel tray and then back to his rubber gloves. He went forward quietly in the silent room on rubber-soled shoes and lifted back the corner of the sheet. The length of drainpipe, the rope, the false teeth, the pebble, the potatoes and the dead fish—in an airproof plastic bag—lay beside the skull and he picked up the drainpipe for a moment, tested its weight in his hands and put it back carefully.

He went to the storeroom and came back with a selection of different capacity specimen bags and slipped the drainpipe carefully into the largest of them, then wrote carefully on the label its general description and file number. He had a very fine copperplate hand—his fountain pen was a silver Lady Sheaffer with curlicues of engraving on its barrel. He took up the false teeth, slipped them into a second bag and labelled them as well.

He picked up the encased fish gingerly and inscribed on its label *Pricanthus niphonius*, the circumstances surrounding its discovery and a separate file number showing it was to be kept refrigerated. The fish and the sweet potatoes would stay in the Mortuary with the skeleton and the teeth; the drainpipe, rope and quartz pebble he slipped into a padded bag to be sent directly around to Yellowthread Street as exhibits.

He went over towards the main doors and dropped the bag into a wire OUT tray to be picked up by the Government mailman. He turned back to look again at the outline under the sheet.

Something disturbed him. He knew he had been thorough. Something niggled at him: he couldn't work out just what it was. Something . . . Something niggled at him . . .

He thought of ringing Harry Feiffer. Feiffer was working on his say-so. He could hear him complaining that if he, the Happy Phantom of the Rue Morgue (oh, he knew what they called him all right) wasn't sure, then how the hell could he, Feiffer, be expected to—

He paused. He felt there was just one more thing he should have done. He grimaced. What was it? Maybe he was simply worrying. He thought, "I don't worry. I'm simply concerned from time to time that the job hasn't been done properly or the result is inconclusive, but I don't *worry*."

There was a letter in the IN mail tray bearing a Russian stamp and his name and address written in a hand unused to the Roman alphabet with the return address—in Russian—a chess club in Moscow. It contained Voroshinsky's latest move in the chess game he and Dawson had been fighting out for the last four months. Dawson touched it with the gloved finger of his right hand and then took it up and flapped it absently in the air.

There was something else . . .

Something.

He looked at the outline of the skeleton under the sheet.

There was something else he should have done for him.

He put the Russian letter in the pocket of his leather apron and pressed the bell for the orderly to remove the skeleton. Strange, he *always* opened postal chess letters immediately, whatever he was doing. They were the one thing he really looked forward to. He analysed his feelings towards it: he really couldn't bring his mind to be interested in Voroshinsky's move one way or the other. And it was the Endgame. He should have been positively shaking with anticipation.

He wasn't.

There was something else he should have done . . .

He couldn't think what it was.

The locking nut for the shotgun was gone! Spencer had the storeroom door open a fraction. He felt around behind him for the locking nut. It was gone. It had rolled away somewhere. He slipped the door closed soundlessly and arced the beam of the flashlight around on the floor. The locking nut was gone. He felt down behind a pile of U.S. dollar exchange rate fluctuations. There was nothing under or around them but dust. It wasn't under the clerk's holey cardigan or near the broken spectacles. It was gone. He flicked out the aerial of the walkie-talkie and pressed down the SEND button. There was nothing. Outside, Yan was gone. In the shop, P. P. Fan was in the process of handing over all his hard-earned cash to three grinning robbers and everything and everyone was gone. Spencer flashed the beam of light desperately up the walls of the storeroom. Nothing. Spider-webs. No spiders. Even the spiders had gone. The shotgun was in pieces. He pushed the door open a fraction and drew his revolver. One of The Deaf and Dumb Gang had his gaze fixed firmly past him towards the street. The starer, like his two companions, had a Japanese Nambu automatic pistol held against his shirt: he looked like he knew how to use it.

P. P. Fan's fingers flicked over his wads of money. He looked down at the note the leader of the gang—a slight lined Northern Chinese in his late forties—had placed before him and failed to marvel at his commercial simplicity.

The note said in one clear, neatly drawn unmistakable character:

MONEY

P. P. Fan forced a grin. For the second time that day he said hopefully, 'All of it?? Not all of it?' He smiled wanly.

The two bandits at the counter looked at him while the other continued staring out towards the street.

P. P. Fan said, 'You're going to leave me enough to get started again? Even bankruptcy court leaves a man enough to—' He looked at the bleak, unsmiling face, 'Aren't you?'

88

The bleak, unsmiling face said, 'Ughmm.'

P. P. Fan said, 'Yes? Is that yes?'

The second bandit—younger and with acne scars on his cheek—glanced at his leader.

The leader said, 'Ughmm.' He looked significantly down at the note on the counter.

Mr Fan followed his eyes. The note said MONEY. Mr Fan said emotionally, 'All of it.'

To come out of the storeroom brandishing a gun would be the surest method of committing suicide in the world. Spencer pushed open the door another inch and got the barrel of his Detective Special in line with the street starer. He thought if he could confuse him he might just be able to get in a shot at his knees before the second bandit realised where the shot had come from. Then, as the first bandit fell, in the mêlée, there was a good chance that . . . Spencer drew a deep breath and shouted out, 'Police! Drop your weapons or I open fire!'

The street starer watched someone walk past the shopfront with interest. The other two bandits nodded to the note again and raised their own weapons a little higher towards Mr Fan's nose level. They glanced at each other. One of them winked: it was going well.

Spencer shouted, 'Police!!'

The acned bandit nudged the starer surreptitiously and when he turned his head winked at him as well: so far so good. The starer smiled faintly and turned back to stare out of the door to the street.

Spencer shouted, *'POLICE!! DROP YOUR WEAPONS!!'*

A voice shouted back at him, a strained voice, the sort of voice that was made when someone had a gun on you and you were still smiling and trying to pretend you weren't shouting at all, *'They're deaf and dumb, you stupid, screaming idiot!'*

Spencer said in spite of himself, 'Really?'

At the counter, P. P. Fan had his head down counting his money. He shouted back through gritted teeth at a picture of Queen Elizabeth the Second's bland visage on an English five pound note, '*Yes!*' The fingers flicked through multi-coloured banknotes, 'Do ... something ... !'

'If I come out there with my gun they'll see me!'

'They're ... taking ... all my ... MONEY!' The lined leader of the gang leaned forward suspiciously and tried to see P. P. Fan's mouth. P. P. Fan passed him over a huge wad of bills and then wrenched another pile from his money drawer. He paused, passed the pile over and went for another, hesitated, rubbed his nose with his hand theatrically and took a large handkerchief from his pocket. He nodded to the lined leader. The lined leader nodded back. P. P. Fan put the handkerchief to his nose and went through the motions of blowing it ferociously. He called out to Spencer through the muffling material, 'Get that policeman who saved me the first time!'

'He's gone! There's only me!'

'Ohh . . .' P. P. Fan transferred the handkerchief to his eyes. 'Help!'

The lined leader took another wad of bills. There were three of them on the counter: a small fortune in the currencies of many nations. He took them to him and nudged the starer. The starer lowered his pistol and produced a paper bag and put the money into it. P. P. Fan called out at the sight of the disappearing lucre, '*Do* something!'

Spencer holstered his revolver. He used the flashlight to look around the room. There was nothing. The shotgun was in pieces. He couldn't simply open fire without warning with the revolver and risk bullets from the Nambus flying out into the street. There were the piles of exchange rates ... the torn cardigan ... the broken glasses ... the shotgun in pieces ... spider's webs. He thought, "They're really deaf and dumb. They're going to let fly at anything or anyone who goes into that shop and if they see a European coming out of the storeroom with a revolver in his hand . . .' He closed his eyes at the thought.

P. P. Fan's voice, muffled in some other way, said, 'I'm going to cut you into a million pieces when I get my hands on you . . .' One of the members of the gang must have looked suspicious. The voice stopped abruptly.

The shotgun barrel was completely detached from the stock. It looked like a long black walking stick. If he had opened fire with the shotgun maybe he could have crippled the three of them with a single blast. But to start off with the .38 shooting 125 grains of solid lead at one target at a time . . . He moved back a little and stood on the broken spectacles. They cracked under his feet. If he could just get to them in the shop without . . .

P. P. Fan's voice said very dismally, as if someone was slowly turning down the volume, 'Well, they've almost finished. I hope you're satisfied with yourself. I don't care any more whether I get twenty years in prison for killing you because as far as I'm concerned . . .' The voice ran out as, presumably, the fingers reached the final, the last, the end, the total desolation of his finances and it all went into the paper bag of a gang of cripples and handicapped, acned, lined and staring . . . P. P. Fan's voice said as its swansong, 'Ohhh . . .'

Spencer pushed open the door and came out. The starer stared at him, and then the acned bandit, nudged by the starer, turned and stared and then, nudged in turn, the lined eyes on the lined leader's face turned to see him. P. P. Fan saw him and thought, "Oh no . . ." and ducked behind the counter. He heard a *click*. (He thought, "That's the first gun being cocked") and then another: *click* (the second piece of deadly weaponry being brought to bear), and then *click-click-click* (He thought, "It's going to be a massacre! My money will be all covered in blood!") and then *click-click-click*. He saw from eye-level with the counter, the first bandit step back and lower his gun, and then, in turn, the second step back and lower his. The starer had gone forward. He had his hand on Spencer's shoulder and was directing him gently towards the counter. P. P. Fan shrieked to himself, "They've all gone mad!" He saw Spencer's face come past the counter, his eyes rolled up into their sockets, showing white, and he thought,

"They've shot him with a silencer and they're gently directing his dead body towards a convenient place to fall." He heard *click-click-click*. ("It's some sort of silenced machine gun and they're shooting him to ribbons!") The starer moved Spencer towards the counter and patted him fraternally on the shoulder. The clicking went on, coming closer.

Spencer stopped. Spencer had the barrel of the gun in his left hand, the breech well up into his coatsleeve, and P. P. Fan thought in an instant of total and awe-struck forgiveness, "The man's a genius!" He got up as the blind European, leaning heavily on his stick, was helped towards the counter by his fraternal sufferer of natural handicaps, the staring deaf and dumb man. The lined leader, in an excess of brotherly love, reached over and took the paper sack from the starer and reached into it to donate a wad of bills to his friend the sightless stick-tapper, then leaned back to stuff it into the poor fellow's pockets, then, simultaneously, looked both shocked and appalled as the frail black walking stick, the sole support of the unfortunate acquaintance upon whom he was about to lavish a share of his hard-gotten gains, transformed itself into twenty-eight inches of best Winchester-proofed steel and with a single arcing blow, knocked him unconscious against Mr Fan's back wall.

The starer stared. His eyes met the muzzle of a snub-nosed revolver held far from blindly in Spencer's other hand and went on staring. The Nambu pistol joined the senseless leader on the floor and was followed a moment later by the acned bandit's gun.

Spencer said, 'Police.'

The starer and the acned man looked blankly at him.

Spencer said clearly and slowly, mouthing the word in Chinese, '*Ging-gwoon*—police officer!'

The two bandits shook their heads.

'Po—lice.' He dropped the shotgun barrel and reached into his coat pocket and showed them his badge.

'Ugghhh . . . mmm . . .'

Spencer said again, 'Police.'

The two bandits gazed at him uncomprehendingly. Spencer said to Mr Fan, 'Write it down.'

Mr Fan wrote down on the back of the MONEY note in Chinese, '*Police. And he's nailed you both cold.*' He leaned over his counter to the starer and exchanged the note with him for the sack of money.

The starer looked down blankly at the piece of paper and then at Spencer. He took a stub of pencil from his shirt pocket and held the note flat in his left hand, then wrote something on it.

Spencer ordered Mr Fan, 'Ring the Station and get some Constables around here.' He stepped forward and kicked the three pistols away towards a back wall. The lined leader was groaning. There was a bad bruise on the side of his head. He reached up and touched it gingerly. He looked at P. P. Fan sadly.

P. P. Fan said in an orgy of admiration. 'Well done! Well done! I take it all back! Well done! Well done!' and went on saying it rhythmically as, one by one, the wads of money went safely back into their drawers. He took the note from the starer, glanced at it, realised it wasn't money, and handed it over to Spencer. He said again, 'Well done! Oh well done! Brilliant young fellow of the obviously rosy and successful future—' He ran out of superlatives. He said decisively, 'What a fine fellow you are, you are,' and thought that was about the acme of what one fellow could say to another who . . . He missed one of the drawers with a wad, checked himself from unseemly hysteria, and babbled, 'Oh, you brilliant young—'

Spencer said for the second time, 'Will you ring the Station!'

'Yes! Yes, of course!' P. P. Fan's fingers raced to the dial. He glanced over at the three members of The Deaf and Dumb Gang, the leader easing himself to his feet, and sneered. He said finally, nodding his head, 'Well done!'

It was only when he was back at the Station that Spencer read the back of the note and the characters the starer had put on it. Judging by the careful calligraphy, they were the only words he knew, and, judging by the way he had written them so clearly and yet so swiftly, words he had written down over and over. Spencer still felt the man's helping hand on his shoulder and the look of astonishment on the lined leader's face in the instant he had been clubbed down.

The commercial, incisive genius of P. P. Fan's read the note over and over. It was evidence. He supposed it should have been kept. He thought he would say at the trial that the note had been lost somewhere on the way to the Station.

He read the note again, by himself for the last time, hiding in one of the toilets of the Police Station and, finally, tore it into shreds and flushed it away.

He saw the characters again for an instant as they were swirled and then swept away in the bowl.

They said simply, *HANDICAPPED. PLEASE HELP.*

. . . he could have sat on the floor and wept.

Farmer Kwok squatted on his haunches by his wooden shack in his sweet potato market garden watching three uniformed Chinese Constables, several coveralled people from Forensic, and one Roman-nosed, chain-smoking Government Medical Officer doing what he dreaded most: digging up his market garden. Where he had unearthed the skeleton and replaced the soil carefully there was now an enormous hole and, where he was planning his next year's crop of sweet potatoes—beginning in his most fertile spot, a few feet from the enormous hole— there was another enormous hole, and, radiating out from it, a desert-like excavation of all the topsoil for ten yards around. Where occasionally he fished to supplement his diet, along a tiny arc of beach in Hop Pei Cove facing his land, there were more Chinese Constables in gumboots sifting through the sand and frightening off the fish. The fact, compared to all this, that they had already searched every square inch of his shack and pried open every nook and cranny in both his tool sheds and ripped his seed boxes into fragments was a mere minor matter, and he thought, "Well, that's me finished. Thank Heaven I'm a bachelor. A few months in a warm prison will at least keep me alive until I can get some help from the Union." He looked over to the tall European in a stained white suit by his car talking on the radio and thought consolingly, "He's right now ordering a room for me in Stanley Prison and making sure they've got enough rice laid on to feed me for the Winter." He picked up a handful of the sandy soil and let it trickle through his fingers.

Feiffer said into the radio telephone, 'They're out here now tearing the place to pieces. I've had a word to Kwok.'

O'Yee's voice said, 'And?'

'And he's in the clear. He dug up the skeleton by accident.' He glanced across to Kwok squatting by his shack and thought he looked a pitiful figure, 'I'm not going to charge him with anything. I think after watching his farm torn to pieces that might be just a bit too much.' Feiffer paused, 'Look, I'm sorry I got irritated when you were calling me at Lee's, Christopher . . .'

'Forget it.' O'Yee said, 'You certainly sound a lot rosier.'

'I am. How about you?'

'Oh, you know, the faithful continue to serve.' He paused. He asked quickly, 'What was the significance of the sweet potatoes on the raft? Offerings to the ghosts?'

'That's it. And the Pricanthus niphonius, the Japanese Big-Eye, was along the same lines. Food for the spirit on its journey. Lew of the Water Police said these people were a superstitious lot. It seems he was right. The rope around the ankles, as Yan pointed out—'

O'Yee said, 'Spencer.'

'What?'

'Spencer. It was Spencer's idea that it was to stop the ghost coming back to haunt. Yan just took the credit for it.'

'Well, whoever. The theory was right. And the drainpipe was an added precaution to make sure the damn thing stayed on the raft and didn't float off. I was going to point out to Kwok that skeletons don't float, but I thought he'd had more than his share of disillusionment for one day so I let it go.' He asked, 'They don't float, do they? They sink.'

'I don't know.' In the Detectives' Room, O'Yee tried to think of movies where there had been skeletons floating around in Davy Jones' locker. Were there any skeletons in *Beneath The Five Mile Reef?* 'I don't know.' *Jaws?* He said, 'Maybe you'd better ask Dawson Baume.' *The Creature From The Black Lagoon . . .?* He said definitely, 'No, they don't. They sink.' He asked, 'Have you found anything new?'

'Not much. The actual grave has been opened and the section of missing finger was there, but apart from that there's nothing. Evidently Kwok had a pretty good dig around when he first found it. Everything he found he put on his home-made raft. I had an idea that we might have found the weapon in one of his tool sheds, or at least the spade that was used to dig the grave in the first place, but since it was twenty years ago anything anyone left lying around has been used non-stop until it fell to pieces in a shower of rust. And anyway, it turns out that Kwok has only been here ten or eleven years and before that the land was waste ground. And naturally, to him that's ancient history and he doesn't know anything about anything.'

There was no reply from the radio.

'Christopher, are you still there?'

'Yes. I was just thinking about something . . .' O'Yee said over-enthusiastically, 'Well, so everything's cleared up, aye?'

'Well at least we know where the skeleton came from. The only question is how it got there in the first place. And now that we know who he was—'

'George Edward Putnam.'

'Right. It's only a matter of slogging away at records to get his address twenty years ago and then running down his friends and acquaintances. Since it was a blow from a blunt instrument and the grave out here wasn't that deep, it's a fair bet it was a spur of the moment job and he was with someone he knew. Find out who he knew and undoubtedly there'll be some sort of personal or domestic motive and if whoever did it is still in the Colony we should have him or her fairly easily.'

He said quickly, 'No, it was a heavy blow and he was tall so it was probably a man.'

'You make it sound easy.'

'Well, it doesn't strike me as particularly difficult.' Feiffer felt relieved. He thought for a moment of the outline under the white sheet. 'Why? There's nothing else, is there?'

'No! No, no, no.'

'What do you mean, No! No, no, no?'

'I mean—' O'Yee thought quickly, 'I mean, I wouldn't want to spoil your victory, that's all.'

'It isn't a victory. It's just routine—why?'

'I mean, I mean . . .' O'Yee said, 'I mean, things seem to be going well for you. I mean, the—the *Jawohl, mein Führer* mood seems to have—' Feiffer could almost hear his brain working overtime over the radio, 'I mean, I just wonder if you've considered every possibility? I mean, what if he was say, a tourist?'

'It's a bit unlikely a tourist would have got his dentures made here. I would have thought if you were going to have to be gummy for a few weeks you'd rather do it, as they say, in the privacy of your own home. It's a pity the dental mechanic didn't put Putnam's address on his chart, but it shouldn't be too hard to find out where he lived.' There was a long silence on the radio. 'Are you still there?' He asked, 'Christopher, do you know something I don't?'

'Me? No! No, no . . .'

'There you go again.' Feiffer said irritably, 'What is it?' Is there a wrinkle in here somewhere? Is that what I'm supposed to deduce?'

'No! No, no . . .'

Feiffer demanded, 'What is it?'

'It's nothing! You've done very well! Nobody could have done better! I'm pleased you're feeling pleased. I wouldn't like you to feel that—' He paused again, 'Well . . .'

'Well what?'

'Well, there is just one tiny little . . .'

'*What?*'

97

'It's—um, well, something to do with the American—'

'It's something to do with the Embassy?'

'Right!'

'Something they told you about the murder?'

'No.'

'Something about Putnam?' Feiffer shouted into the handset, 'What the hell is this, Twenty Questions?'

'They said something about Putnam.'

'Well? Come on—out with it.'

There was another silence. Feiffer said into the telephone ominously, 'Christopher . . .'

'Oh, by the way, Spencer got The Deaf and Dumb Gang. That's great, isn't it?'

'What has that got to do with this?'

'Nothing. Nothing at all. I—I just thought you might like to know, that's all . . .'

'Well, I don't want to know! But I'm very happy for him! Good for him! Well done! Terrific! Hoo-ray! *Now what the hell did the Embassy say about Putnam?*'

In the Detectives' Room, O'Yee looked for the cat. In preparation for nuclear war, it was well bunkered behind the piles of folders. O'Yee felt his finger on the button: the nuclear war was about to start. He shivered in the ninety-eight degree temperature from the happily fissioning radiator, closed his eyes and said carefully and very slowly, 'Harry, your twenty year old skeleton on the raft . . . your George Edward Putnam . . . according to the American Embassy . . .' He drew a breath.

'*Yes?*'

O'Yee said evenly into the telephone, 'Harry, he's still alive.'

9

'What the hell do you mean, "he's still alive"?' In the Detectives' Room Feiffer slammed the door behind him, was met by a fiery blast from the radiator and jerked the door back open again. Auden was in his shirtsleeves saying happily to Spencer, 'Superior brainpower. He met his match, that's all . . .' Feiffer demanded for the second time, 'What do you mean?'

O'Yee gazed up at him from behind his reading glasses. 'He's still alive, that's what I mean. The Embassy says his passport is current and he's still alive.' He smiled sheepishly.

Auden, oblivious, went on to Spencer at a side desk, 'Deduction, that's what it was. When everything possible has been eliminated, the solution has to be the *impossible*.' He said proudly, 'That's Sherlock Holmes.' He flicked his gaze to Feiffer, 'I got the mugger, Harry, did I tell you?'

'Passports can be faked. Didn't you ever read *The Day of the Jackal*?'

'Not American passports.' O'Yee said in that rising San Franciscan accent, 'British passports may be able to be faked, but not American ones.'

'Why not? All you have to do is pick the name of a dead person, forge a verification reference and—'

O'Yee said, 'And in the case of American passports, turn up at the Embassy and have a Consular official compare your face with the one on the photo and have yourself checked through God knows how many computers linked directly to

Washington.' O'Yee said patriotically, 'You can't even get a visa into the country without having your birthmarks checked, let alone a *passport*.'

'I'm not impressed.'

Auden gave up waiting for admiration from Feiffer and turned back to admiration from Spencer. He said quietly, understandingly, 'I appreciate that you got The Deaf and Dumb Gang, Bill, but that was just pure stand-over stuff. Violence. The modern detective has to use his noodle to get results. The gallop and gunshot boys have all gone. We're in the era of the intelligent criminal and you have to—'

Feiffer said, 'Will you shut up!' The radiator gave another gust of infernal heat and he kicked it to one side. (O'Yee looked shocked.) 'I'm not impressed. It's still perfectly possible for someone to take Putnam's identity, America computer-land or not.'

O'Yee said quietly, 'And just turn up every five years or so to have his passport renewed?'

'Correct.'

'And for the rest of the time, as they say, keep a low profile. I mean, you wouldn't want to make a career out of Putnam, would you?' O'Yee said, 'Like, I mean, register yourself with the same American Embassy and the Treasury Department and the Internal Revenue Service—'

'What are you getting at?'

O'Yee said simply, 'Putnam pays taxes.'

'To whom?'

'To America. The Embassy checked that too. They won't issue a passport unless your tax situation is up to date with Washington—and Putnam's is.' He paused, 'I'm sorry, Harry, I don't know who your skeleton was, but it sure wasn't someone called George Edward Putnam.'

'Then who the hell is it?'

Auden went on in a whisper, 'This fellow, Ong, now. Now he thought that he was a fairly bright cookie—and, to be fair, when he was only dealing with dumb uniformed cops and with his victims, I suppose—to give him his due—you could say he was pretty good. But, then, aha, brought up against a clear modern mind—'

Spencer said, 'It certainly does sound like good work, Phil.'

'Oh, I'm not putting your bit down. The old D and D Gang, they weren't exactly—' Auden said confidentially, 'But you've got to admit, they were a bit obvious, weren't they? No, you've got to outwit your modern criminal and put the fear of God into him. He's got to know right from the start that you're smarter than he is. He's got to know that you can get him any time you want—any tick of the clock.' He said grandly, 'I'm not even opposing bail on this fellow Ong. Why should I? Let him go back home and stew until the case comes up. He's not going to run because he knows that *any tick of the clock* I can get him—any old tick.' He said, 'Your people have got to be kept in custody, right?'

'Well actually, I thought I wouldn't oppose bail . . .'

'*Why not?*'

'Well, I suppose . . .' Spencer said softly, 'To tell you the truth, Phil, I suppose I feel a bit sorry for them . . .'

'YOU WHAT?'

Feiffer said, 'Auden, shut up!' He turned to O'Yee, glanced at the radiator for an annoyed moment, thought to say something, then changed his mind, 'All right, Christopher, he's still alive. Let's say for the time being that I accept what the Embassy says.' He saw O'Yee about to give him a burst of Old Glory patriotism, 'All right, let's just say I accept it full stop. However, the mere fact that he has been indentified as Putnam —courtesy of the false teeth and whatnot—does tend to suggest that there's some connection between whoever it is—'

Spencer said helpfully, 'Phlebas the Phoenician.'

Auden looked at him.

Feiffer said, 'Pardon?'

Spencer quoted,

'Phlebas the Phoenician, a fortnight dead,
Forgot the cry of gulls and the deep sea swell
And the profit and loss.
          A current under sea

Picked his bones in whispers. As he rose and fell . . .'

He said, 'T. S. Eliot.' He waited expectantly.

Feiffer said, 'John Doe. Let's assume Putnam alive or dead has some sort of causal relationship with the fact that—' he glanced at Spencer. Spencer looked hurt. 'That Phlebas was found dead in the ground, all right? So let's find where Putnam hangs out, and go and have a chat to him. Has the American Embassy got an address on him?' He said quickly before O'Yee could answer, 'Of course the American Embassy has got an address on him. What is it?'

'It's a Hong Kong box number. I've run it down through the Post Office and the owner resides at Number Six, Wood-carvers' Road, Hong Bay. I then got in touch with Directory Enquiries and got their reverse address listings and Number Six, Woodcarvers' Road is a business office called W & P Enterprises.' He added efficiently, 'And then I got in touch with the financial correspondent of the local newspaper and W & P Enterprises is a bar called *The Crap Game*. He drew a breath, 'I then rang Companies House and it's a bar called *The Crap Game* jointly owned by two Americans residing in Hong Kong called Charlie Weale and—guess what the P stands for?'

Feiffer glanced at Spencer. Spencer forbore saying, 'Phlebas.' Feiffer said, 'Putnam.'

'Right. I *then*, rang the tourist office and asked them about said *Crap Game* and I discovered that they do quite a good Singapore gin sling.' He said with a trace of annoyance at the way Feiffer was glaring at the burning radiator, 'And at that point, O Master, I thought I'd done my bit for the day. I know it's hot in here.'

Auden said, 'It is hot. Why don't you turn the bloody thing off?'

'Because I can't turn the bloody thing off! Why the hell is everyone getting at me?' He turned his gaze to Feiffer, 'What's so important about this job anyway? It's just a pile of bones. Why don't we just—'

Feiffer said, 'Because he was murdered!'

'Lots of people get murdered!' O'Yee said, 'What did Dawson Baume do to you anyway?'

'He didn't do anything to me. The fact that someone has been dead for twenty years doesn't diminish anything.' Feiffer looked at Auden and Spencer, 'And since you two appear to have single-handedly cleared up the entire current crimewave in Hong Bay' (Auden nodded enthusiastically) 'I don't see why we shouldn't spend the time to clear Putnam from our books.'

O'Yee cut in correctively, 'It isn't Putnam.'

'All the better. Whoever it is.' He addressed the broiling room, 'Doesn't anyone *care* that this poor bastard got his head bashed in? He wasn't just some sort of articulated bone-man the fishes pushed up onto the shore you know, he was a person. I fail to understand why everyone seems to think it's just some sort of joke.'

'Harry, it was twenty years ago.'

'So what? If someone brained me with a blunt instrument I think I'd care to be thought important even if it was two hundred years ago—' He said finally, 'What's the use? Poor old whatever-his-name was doesn't amount to anything, does he? Putnam or John Doe or—'

Spencer said helpfully, 'Phlebas.'

Auden finally remembered a name he had been trying to think of all day. He said triumphantly to Spencer, 'Poirot!' He raised his finger to Spencer to fix the point, 'Now he was just the sort of detective I was—' He caught Feiffer's eye and stopped. He said fraternally, 'Mind you, I think the boss is right. This character Putnam or whoever, it could be just the sort of difficult puzzle a professional detective could really get interested in. It seems to me now . . .' he paused for reflective deduction, 'That, given the circumstances of an uncertain indentification . . .' He looked at Spencer expectantly like a schoolmaster leading a dense child, 'Now, Bill, what would you say your very first move in this . . .' He saw Feiffer's eyes for the second time, 'I'm only trying to help!'

O'Yee's phone rang. He shook his head sagely. 'Well,

Harry, I hope you can justify chasing after a twenty year corpse if anyone in authority asks you about it. If you want my opinion—' The phone rang insistently and he picked it up, 'Detectives' Room.' The Commander's voice roared down the line, 'What the hell is going on there? Half my people are out at a market garden in Hop Pei Cove. Is that O'Yee?'

'Yes, sir.' O'Yee paused for a moment while the Commander drew breath for the full tirade. He said into the phone, 'Just one moment, please, sir.' He smiled pleasantly and held up the phone above his head. He said evenly, 'Harry, I believe it's for you.'

The Commander said ominously, 'I want to know just what the devil is going on out there.'

'I don't know what you mean, sir.'

'Yes, you do. Oh, yes, you do, North Point have got a double homicide up in their district and, quite rightly, they rang Forensic to get some help on it. Forensic are all out carving out trenches in sweet potato farms. O.K. So they rang the Government Medical Officer so he could examine the bodies and—guess what? The Government Medical Officer is out in the same potato farm picking around in the muck looking for twenty year old buried bones. O.K. So they thought they'd get on to the Government Undertaker to get the bodies carted away. The Government Undertaker is standing by at the potato farm in case they find—what? More bones. They rang the Mortuary and guess what? The bones are already there. All of them. One complete skeleton. So what is everyone looking for?' He exploded, 'And I've had some Communist idiot on the phone raving about his cousin claiming that he isn't his cousin at all and it's just part of a capitalist conspiracy on the part of the police to corrupt the workers and bring the good name of socialism into vile repute—and guess which Union he represents? *The same fucking Union that handles the affairs of sweet potato farmers who have bones on their properties!*' The voice said, quivering, 'I don't know why you're doing this to me, Harry. I've been trying to think in what way I've given rise to such feelings of unmerciful revenge in you, Harry, but I can't. And it's making me more than a bit twitchy.' He roared down the line, 'AND, HARRY, WHEN I TWITCH, MERE DETECTIVE CHIEF INSPECTORS TREMBLE!'

'I'm sorry you feel that way, Neal.'

'Don't you call me "Neal"! For some reason unbeknown to me, Feiffer, you've decided you're out to get me! And the American Embassy rang me not fifteen minutes ago and demanded to know if there was going to be full diplomatic clearance on an investigation of one of their citizens. Now, I'm going to ask you one more time—very calmly, very profession-ally, very detachedly, without the faintest tinge of paranoia in my voice, What the blue blazes are you doing down there?' He paused, 'Well? Well? *WELL!*'

'We're investigating a murder.'

'Well, thank God for that! I'd hate to think all this was for nothing more than a fucking *traffic ticket*! What murder! ?'

'A John Doe murder.'

Spencer said softly, 'Phlebas . . .' He saw Auden slink over towards the files and look at them casually, Hercule Poirot on the track of a long forgotten perfect crime that he could crack for the Western world while mere mortals made telephone calls. He said suddenly, 'Hey, there's a dead cat behind here!'

The Commander's voice took a calm-before-the-storm quietude, 'Good. A John Doe murder. Good. Good, Harry. Go on please.'

O'Yee said, 'Leave it alone.'

'It's dead.' Auden poked at the files with his finger. 'It's come in here and died.'

'It isn't dead!'

'The heat's killed it.'

'The heat hasn't bloody killed it. It came in here to get warm!' O'Yee warned Auden, 'You keep away from that cat.'

'Harry, I'm waiting . . . now, more details, please?'

'We don't have any.'

'I see. You don't have any more details. Good. Good. I'm feeling better already. All this hard, solid information is really putting me in the picture. A murder. John Doe. No indentification. Now where do the old bones fit in, Harry?'

'They're the victim.' Feiffer said, 'The victim was found in skeleton form.'

'I see. A burn case or a bride in the acid bath job. Something like that? And you dug the bones up in—'

'No, he floated in.'

Over the phone, Feiffer heard, actually *heard*, the Commander blink.

'The skeleton floated in, Harry?' The Commander's voice said quietly, 'Harry, skeletons don't float . . .'

'No, sir. He came in on a raft.'

Auden said definitely, 'This cat is bloody dead!' He poked it with a pencil and the cat clawed him across the knuckles. He said, 'Oww!'

'What was that, Harry? Was that someone calling for help in your police station?'

'No, sir. One of my men was just scratched by a cat.'

'A cat? Oh, I see, Harry, the skeleton's cat, no doubt?'

'A different cat.'

'I don't want to know about the cat, Harry.' The voice balanced precariously like Blondin above Niagara Falls. The water below the balancing Blondin was labelled TOTAL INSANITY. 'And how did this skeleton come in on a raft, Harry?'

'He was dug up and put on it, sir, and he came back in and . . . and we found him . . .'

'And how long has he been dead?'

'Twenty years.'

'I see. And where do the Americans come into this? Was he an American?'

'Apparently not.'

'Then why is the American Embassy ringing me, Harry?'

'We thought it was an American named Putnam. But he—' he glanced unconvinced at O'Yee, 'But he may not be, sir. We thought he was the owner of a bar in Woodcarvers' Road but apparently he wasn't. I'm going out there now to talk to him.'

'The skeleton?'

'The owner of the bar, sir.'

There was a clicking sound at the other end of the line as if, Captain Queeg-like, the Commander had picked up two or three little metal balls from his desk and was rolling them obsessionally between his fingers.

Feiffer said, 'I would like to carry on with this one, Commander. If you'll authorise it.'

There was silence.

Feiffer said, 'Commander?'

'Oh, yes! Why not? Delighted. Entranced. Overjoyed. All yours? Yes, of course, dear boy. Every time someone rings me up about this or when the men come in their green cart to take me away to the Funny Farm I shall be absolutely chuffed to say, "Oh, no, I don't know anything about this at all—it's good old Harry Feiffer's." Of course. My pleasure.' He paused and asked in a strange thin voice, 'Anything on the mugger or The Deaf and Dumb Gang? Too much to ask? Forgive me for asking.'

'We got them all.'

'Oh, really?' There seemed to be a faint crackle beginning somewhere in the back of the Commander's throat, 'Oh. Oh, good. How clever of you all. Thank you so much. You got The Deaf and Dumb Gang . . . well, well, well. How?'

Feiffer said evenly, 'One of my detectives pretended he was blind.'

'Oh! Of course! How crass of me. How else do you get a gang of people who are deaf and dumb? You pretend you're blind.' He said, 'And I'm not even going to ask how you got a mugger who mugged people on an invisible floor, because, to be totally candid with you, Harry, I don't think my poor brain could withstand the answer.' He said in an eerie tone, 'I've been looking at my desk calendar and I've only got a few more years until I retire. Won't that be nice? I can grow roses in the grounds of the asylum. I'm looking forward to that.'

He said in a warm friendly voice, like a distant uncle wishing Merry Christmas to the least favourite of his hydrocephalic nephews, 'Good bye now, Harry, and my very best wishes to you and yours. Goodbye.'

The line clicked off very softly.

Feiffer cleared his throat and looked around the room. There was silence. Auden nursed his knuckles. Feiffer said lamely, 'Well, if he's using someone else's passport it's fraud, isn't it? That makes it current. Doesn't it?' He said quietly, 'That was the Commander. We've got the go-ahead to carry on.' He saw Auden pouting that the merits of Poirot hadn't been sung to the highest, 'He said getting the mugger and The Deaf and Dumb Gang was good work.' He looked at O'Yee. Pouting faces everywhere. There was a slight dent in the radiator where he had kicked it. 'Well . . .' He shivered slightly and winked at the radiator. 'Well, all together now . . .' Even the radiator looked only half-hearted. It gurgled miserably.

He smiled to all and sundry, patted the radiator affectionately, and, as inconspicuously as possible, beat a hasty retreat out the door.

salu'brious a. Healthy (chiefly of climate, air, etc.
Hence or cogn. ~LY adv., salubrity n., –lŏŏ–,
–lū–). L *salubris*.

seedy a.   Full of seed, going to seed; (of brandy)
having flavour attributed to weeds along the vines;
(colloq.) shabby-looking . . .

Balanced abjectly and adjectivally midway between the two
stood Woodcarvers' Road, Hong Bay. It was a balance fostered
chiefly by the most prominent long-term institutions in the
place: on one hand, the woodcarvers and the bars (the twin
earners of the seedy sobriquet), and, on the other, the new-
fangled creeping salubrity of a more recent arrival, the Hong
Bay Peoples' Middle School at the corner of Jade Road. The
Communists who ran the school, it was well-known and
demonstrable (each of the pro-seedy woodcarvers and bar
owners carried proven mental equation of the ratio between
seediness and tourist attraction committed indelibly to memory)
were people of austerity and incorruptible plainness. Their
view of a street in which the cadres of the future were to be
nurtured would have been to cement it all over into grey
monolithic blocks, paper the blocks with inspiring pictures of
peasants laughing and looking determined on tractors, and
then, rewriting history, forget the woodcarvers and bars ever
existed in the place. Selected visiting groups of Albanian coal-

miners and English fellow-travellers would then be invited to view the blocks and the pictures and the re-written history with the appropriate gasps of approval before going on to the school itself to see the new youth of the Red East at their sums and hear a recorded three-hour speech of welcome from fraternal organisations in Peking.

The woodcarvers and bar owners on the other hand, being unrepentant capitalists, had no such noble urges for change. It was well known that tourists who listened to three-hour speeches and gazed at monolithic cement blocks had been observed over a long period of time to keep their hands firmly away from their wallets. Austerity meant boredom. Seediness meant bargains. A battle of urban landscaping raged daily. Wall posters exhorting the end of the capitalist system appeared overnight on top of carefully-lettered placards in English pointing out that Mr Yung the Woodcarver gave the best low-rent based camphorwood carved bargains in Hong Kong—and were immediately torn down again by Mr Yung—topless photographs of the well-known Australian stripper Robin Redbreasts were covered over—a red starred hat was painted on her peroxided hair and her main assets cloaked in a representation of a people's militia tunic—carefully placed garbage and seedy wall-decorations (usually the current crop of WANTED posters supplied to one of the bar owners by a sympathetic brother-in-law in the Constabulary) were removed and replaced by charts of the latest steel production figures, and on the very worst occasions, little groups of clear-eyed children gathered to sing patriotic songs and collar passing Americans in order to deliver them a carefully rehearsed sibilant lecture on the evils of drink and capitalism as it sapped and corrupted the morals of all those who indulged in it.

On such occasions it had been known for the local bar owners to call in the quenching services of the local gutter hosing truck from the Street Cleansing Department. At which point it had been known for the Communists to call in the services of baseball bats. At which point the secret societies were called in with razors and zip-guns. At which point, when the going got really tough . . . well, it had happened once anyway . . . the *police* arrived.

The Crap Game was at the end of Woodcarvers' Road, in a prime position as far away as possible from the Communist school and, the other traders in the street had observed enviously on more than one occasion, by the time the luckless tourist had worked his way past chanting youths, painted-over topless ladies, the exhortations of grinning tractor-borne agrarian workers, the garbage whether on view or at one side of the road, the cruising vehicles of the cleansing department, the triad personnel carriers and the occasional police car and had bartered, purchased and arranged to ship back to Ohio one or several of Mr Yung's camphorwood chests together with nests of carved tables from his competitors, he, the luckless tourist, was more than ready to pay almost anything for a drink.

At the door, Feiffer looked around the bar. If the place had been founded on a crap game it must have been a legendary one. There must have been three hundred wrist watches lining the walls, together with rings, brooches, pendants, gold coins, key chains, medals, hair clips, belt knuckles, wallets, credit cards, bill clips—in fact almost everything a man could carry on his person or pin or clip or affix onto his clothing or load into his pockets, and anything which, in a moment of desperation, knowing the dice would roll right for him this one final time, he could convince his wife, girlfriend, mother or sister to part with on the absolute certainty that this time nothing could go wrong and the pot—*God, look at the size of it!*—would come his way. The shaven-headed barman, wiping down the counter top with a towel marked HONG KONG HILTON said lazily, 'You're a cop.' The rest of the bar was empty. He glanced around and lit a long cigarette from a pack under the counter, 'Before you ask, no, I'm not running a poker school and no, I've never heard of the local floating crap game and no, I don't have any roulette wheels or forms of amusement in the back room or upstairs. Feel free to check.' He went back to wiping the counter. 'William Charles Weale, bar licence number 49863 dash 35, current and paid up.'

Feiffer said, 'Harry Feiffer.' He walked forward and sat on a stool facing the bar.

'The pleasure's all yours.' The eyes stayed on the delicate operation of wiping down a perfectly clean counter, 'Before you ask, all the stuff you see on the walls is legally mine.'

'Where did you get it all?'

'Where do you think I got it?'

'I would have thought the decorator supplied it.' Feiffer said easily, 'I notice all the wallets look like they've never been carried in a pocket in their lives and the credit cards all have an S on them.' He saw Weale's glistening pate. 'For Specimen.'

'Don't tell me, let me guess. You're a detective.'

'And you are the joint owner of W & P Enterprises with George Edward Putnam.'

'What do you want?'

'I want George Edward Putnam.'

'He's not here.' Weale finished with the bar and looked up. He had a bland, almost featureless face. 'O.K. so I believe you're not from the Vice or Gaming. So what do you want Eddie for?'

'Is that what he's called?'

'Sure. What's he done this time?'

'That depends. What did he do last time?' (Weale reached over for a whisky bottle and put it on the counter. Feiffer shook his head.) How long have you known him?'

Weale released a long slow breath. 'A long time. We won the stake for this place in a crap game on a ship in harbour.' He made a tired smile, 'Outside the legal limits. Before that we were in Korea together.' He shrugged, 'And I knew him at home in Alabama. I've—' the face faded—'I've known that sonofabitch for it seems like about two hundred years. Why do you want to know?' He looked down and took up the bar towel again to resume wiping.

'He may be dead.'

'Yeah? Great! How did it happen? That—*bastard*! You want me to identify the body, right? Day or night, buddy, day or night . . . What did he die of? Heart attack? That bastard was as strong as an ox. Jesus, as strong as a fugging bloodsucker. I didn't even know he was back.'

'From—' Weale said abruptly, 'Where is he? Is he back here in Hong Kong?'

Feiffer nodded.

'Macao. He lives in Macao. Once a fugging year I send him his share of the profits.' He said happily to himself, 'And now the bastard's dead? Well, that's a good roll if ever I saw one. Terrific!' He asked suddenly, 'What do you mean, he *may* be dead? Is he or isn't he?'

'We don't know if it's him or not.'

'I'll identify him for you.'

'You can't.'

'Don't you believe it! That bastard's face is engraved on my brain!'

'What did he do to you anyway?'

'What did he do to me? He staked me to half a roll and then when it came up and we cleaned the game out he came up with the idea that we should stay on in Hong Kong and open a bar and we should be fifty-fifty partners and then— just wait for it—the moment the papers were drawn up and signed he told me there was nothing in them to say he had to *work* for his fifty split so he took off.' He said vehemently, 'And that mother's been collecting from me every year on the dot since that day and he hasn't done an hour's labour for it. That's what he did to me. Lead me to the nearest morgue, lift up the sheet on your cadaver and after that the drinks are on the house.'

'Did you have an inheritance clause written into the contract?'

'You're damn right!' Weale stopped. He said suddenly, appalled, 'Jesus, the bastard wasn't murdered, was he? Christ, I didn't do it!'

'We have reason to believe—'

'Christ! What the hell have I been saying?'

'We're not certain it is Putnam at the moment.'

'Listen, Mr—'

'Feiffer.'

'Listen, Mr Feiffer—'

'Did he pay taxes on the money you gave him?'

'How do I know if he paid taxes? Listen, just because I hated the guy doesn't mean I—'

'No one's accusing you of anything. I'm just trying to establish his identity. We found the body in—in a decomposed state. There's no question of anyone being able to identify him by sight. He was found in Hop Pei Cove.'

'In the water?'

'More or less. But if you've been in contact with him recently the possibility is that the man we found isn't Putnam at all. I'm just trying to find out when he was last—'

'I last gave him his cut in June.'

'June this year?'

'Sure. The cheque was cashed.' Weale asked, 'So was it him? Was there something on him? Some ID or—'

'There wasn't anything.'

'So how do you know it's Eddie Putnam?'

'It obviously isn't Eddie Putnam.' Feiffer got up from the stool, 'I seem to have spoiled your day. The body was found in skeleton form.'

'Jesus! How long had he been dead?'

'Quite a while. But if you saw him alive in June this year it can hardly be him.' Feiffer said, 'Thanks anyway—' He turned to go.

'I didn't see him.'

'What did you say?'

'I said, I didn't see him. I sent the money.'

'To where?'

'To his bank in Macao. The Prosperity. I didn't say I'd seen him. I just sent him the cheque.' Weale said, 'I don't know how long your skeleton's been dead, but I haven't seen Putnam since the day we got the contracts signed.'

'How many years?'

'How many years what?' Weale said quietly, 'Jesus, it's him, isn't it? The bastard's finally got his claws out of me. He's dead. It's fugging Putnam, isn't it? Someone finally killed him.'

'That depends on how long ago you saw him. Three years ago?'

'Is that when he died?'

Feiffer said, 'Five? Maybe ten? When was the last time you saw him alive?'

'Oh, I get it: all I've got to do is pick a number and if the thing was dead before that then it can't have been Putnam, right? The old guessing game.'

'Something like that.'

'Then you're out of luck, Jack.'

'Why?'

'Because I haven't seen good old Eddie Putnam since the day the contract was signed. And it's for sure your skeleton hasn't been dead that long.' Weale said mournfully, 'Well, it was a nice thought and you almost made me a free man—'

'How long ago did you see him?'

'How long's he been dead?'

Feiffer smiled at him, 'You first.'

Weale said, 'O.K. Twenty fugging years! Now how long has the thing been dead? Two years? Three? Six fugging months—?' He saw Feiffer's face change. 'Is that it? Did I pick the right—' He said in a gasp, '*Jesus Christ!*'

Feiffer said quietly, 'Congratulations.'

Weale's mouth had fallen open. He reached for the whisky bottle on the counter with a trembling hand.

He said incredulously, 'Well, Jesus *Christ!*'

He shook his head in total and complete astonishment.

Feiffer came into the Detectives' Room and went directly for the Macao phone book. He opened it and began searching for a number in the intricacies of the Portuguese listings. O'Yee said, 'Did you see Weale?'

Feiffer nodded. He turned over a page and began running his finger down a series of sub-listings for Macao government departments.

'What's he like?'

He found a number, considered it for a moment, then moved the finger on. 'A sort of overweight Yul Brynner.'

'But he was Putnam's partner? He was the right one?'

'Yes, he was the right one.' The listings seemed to go on interminably. You needed to be a United Nations linguist to even work out which department was which.

'Did he know anything—about Putnam?'

'Yes.'

'And?'

Feiffer found the right number. He scribbled it down on the phone book before it escaped back into the maze of Romance languages. 'And he's dead.'

'Who? Weale?'

'No. Putnam.'

'He's dead?'

Feiffer nodded and began dialling the number.

O'Yee said, 'Again?'

Captain Augusto Chagas of the Portuguese Colonial Police in Macao, the product of an Oporto wine-growing farmer and a Cambridge wine-tippling mother, said urbanely down the line in perfect English, 'Harry, dear boy . . .' He chuckled to himself. 'I'm Captain Louis Renault again, I'm afraid. That movie's been on again at the *Estoril*. It's the fifth time this week I've seen it. Ah, Ingrid Bergmann . . .'

'How did you manage it this time?'

Chagas' voice said, 'Oh, the army of fans is growing here, you know. It gets easier every time. One of these days I expect it'll even be shown completely and solely by popular demand. On this particular occasion the Bishop here put in a complaint about the number of sex films being shown in Macao, and, as a good son of Holy Mother Church, I felt it my duty to confiscate three cans of *Concentration Camp*

Chorus Girl and have them publicaly burned. Being, none-theless, *a human man*, at the same time, I took pity on the unfortunate cinema owner to whom the forces of greed and sexual exploitation had supplied the offending film, and I arranged to have a substitute brought in for him at great expense from a distributor in Tokyo with whom I have con-nections: *Star Wars*. However, at almost the last moment, there was a little trouble with Customs—nothing important, just a routine query from the police, don't you know—and the harassed cinema owner was forced to look around urgently for yet another substitute. Fortunately, the same Macao police had a copy of rather a good film—if a little dated by some standards—that I personally seized from a cruise liner on which we suspected narcotics and I—to the cinema owner's eternal gratitude—supplied it to him free of charge.' He said to himself coo-ingly, '*Casablanca*—What a film. It's the twenty-third time it's been shown in Macao this year alone.'

'Amazing.'

'Isn't it?' The Iberian Claude Rains cleared his throat, 'Well, what can we do for you?'

'Do you know the Prosperity Bank there?'

'Sure.'

'Is it respectable?'

'Highly. Why? Has something funny been—'

'I'd just like you to go around there if you would, Augusto, and—'

Chagas said warningly, 'Whooa, Harry, Macao banks won't tell you anything about anything. Even with a Court Order. And you won't get one. I think if you want to get the state of an account from them your best plan is to—'

'I don't want the state of an account. I just want the description of a man who draws on it.'

'And his name presumably. They won't give it to you.'

'I know the name. The name is George Edward Putnam. All I want to know is what George Edward Putnam looks like. I think they should be able to manage that. Also, I'd like you to go through your files and see if you can come up with an address on this Putnam.'

'He lives here?'

'Yes.'

'Then that shouldn't be too difficult. What's he done exactly?'

'Exactly, he hasn't done anything. Exactly, I'm inclined to think he's dead.'

'And this person who's using his account is an impostor?'

'Yes.'

'And you want me to check the address and see if there are any signs of a body. Right?'

'We've got the body. I want to see who's living there, if anyone. We've got a description of the real Putnam from the American Embassy here and I want to compare the two.'

There was a pause from the Macao end.

'Are you still there?'

'Yes.' Chagas said absently, 'I'm . . . just going through the list of foreign residents presently registered in Macao . . . American nationals . . . I happened to have it on my desk and . . . ' His voice sharpened as he came to the end of the list, 'And there's no one by that name. Of course, if your man is a recent arrival . . .'

'To the best of my knowledge he's been there twenty years.'

'You're sure he isn't just a visitor? I can check the immigration records for you and see when he came in and out if you like.'

'If you could.'

'Sure. When do you want me to get back to you about it?'

'When's the next showing of *Casablanca*?'

'In exactly ninety-three minutes.'

'And of course, about then you're going to suddenly develop the most awful migraine headache and have to go home early. Right?'

'Malaria, as a matter of fact. There's an early morning showing tomorrow and then another in the afternoon.

Migraine headaches don't usually last that long.' He offered, 'Should I busy myself with the records in the next sixty minutes or wait until after my attack has passed?'

'Before.'

'Done.' Chagas said pleasantly, 'Well, I'll get on with it. I'm beginning to feel a little under the weather already. Always a pleasure to talk to the Hong Kong police. If there's ever anything else we can do for you I'm always only too glad to—' he paused for a moment, 'Well, you know . . . round up the usual suspects.'

At the other end of the line, Feiffer smiled. He said softly, 'Louis, I have the feeling this could be the beginning of a beautiful friendship . . .'

He heard Chagas chortling as he replaced the receiver.

O'Yee read aloud from a photostat of Putnam's passport application, ' "George Edward Putnam, born Nelson, Alabama, April 7th, 1925. Parents, Edward R. Putnam and Mary K. Putnam (née Robertson), both deceased. Height five foot eleven; hair, brown; eyes, brown; full beard; distinguishing characteristics nil." And that's it. I've asked the Embassy to telex Washington for his Army record. Passport up to date, taxes paid, address and box number in Hong Kong, no criminal convictions—and that's it. He asked, "How tall was your skeleton?" '

'Five foot eleven.'

'Lots of people are five foot eleven.'

The phone rang and Feiffer picked it up quickly. Chagas' voice at the other end of the line said, 'I'll have to make this quick, I've just come down with the preliminary stages of a minor recurrence of malaria.'

'I'm very sorry to hear that.' There was a click as the telephonist in Macao police headquarters withdrew the plug. 'Did you go around to the bank?'

'I rang them. I spoke to one of the Chinese tellers. You do know, of course, Harry, that this fellow Putnam only goes into that bank once a year?'

'Yes, I knew that.'

'Well, in that case you obviously can't expect much of a description. No one seemed to remember him except this one teller. Evidently Putnam had some sort of very pronounced Deep South accent and no one could quite understand him. The teller who remembered him spent some time in Virginia or somewhere and he was the only one who could work out what he was saying.' He asked, 'Where was your real Putnam from?'

'Alabama, in the Deep South.'

'Ah-ha, someone's done their homework. And whoever it was, he certainly doesn't live here under the name of Putnam. And he doesn't visit under that name either. The computer tells me there's no record of anyone named George Edward Putnam, U.S. citizen, ever having presented himself at the port of entry, or having left. How does he identify himself at the bank? They didn't tell me.'

'He presents his passport.'

Chagas said, interested, 'Does he? Then he must have at least a superficial resemblance to the real Putnam if nothing else. In any event, I've got a description for you, such as it is. It's pretty general. Do you want to match it with yours as we go?'

'Fine.' Feiffer said, 'Height. I've got five foot eleven.'

'Five foot eleven, six foot. The same.'

'Eyes?'

Chagas said, 'Brown. And the real Putnam?'

'Brown. Hair?'

'Brown. And brown full beard.' Chagas waited interrogatively.

'Ditto.'

'Distinguishing marks?'

Feiffer said, 'None.'

'Then, as you say, ditto. Have you got his age, Harry?'

'He'd be about mid-fifties.'

'So is the man who collects the money.' Chagas said encouragingly, 'Still, that description could fit a lot of people.'

'People whose faces match someone else's on a passport?'

'Passports can be forged. Have you got his photograph?'

'I've got a photostat of the copy the American Embassy has. It's blurred. The usual sort of passport picture. With the beard it could be almost anybody.'

Chagas said thoughtfully, 'Yeah.' He brightened up, 'I'll be around here for another thirty minutes or so. The teller's having a cogitate about it and if he thinks of anything else he'll ring and tell me. Is there anything else at all you know about Putnam?'

'Not a bloody thing!'

'So is it him or not?'

'I wish I knew.'

'Sorry I couldn't do any better.' Chagas said grandly, 'I wouldn't say this to anyone else, but if there's anything else, you can ring the cinema number'—he gave it to Feiffer—'and if it's urgent my malaria might pass. In the meantime—'

'In the meantime, enjoy your film.' There was a click as the telephonist inserted her plug to check if the call was over.

With the ability and ease of Claude Rains doing the simplest of all simple scenes, for her benefit, Chagas groaned a malarial groan.

Two phones rang simultaneously. O'Yee picked his up and said, 'Detectives' Room.' He heard Feiffer say, 'This is Feiffer. Yes, Mr Weale?' as Chagas shouted behind a background noise of traffic, 'Ah, Christopher, I'm just outside a cinema. I dropped into the Prosperity Bank on the way. It was just a few doors down...'

Feiffer said, 'I appreciate that, Mr Weale.' He smiled to himself, 'No, I do appreciate your interest . . . sure. Any information you might be able to give would be very . . . no, the description so far is reasonably inadequate.' He answered guardedly, 'No, I'm afraid we're not in a position to say what it was we found with the skeleton that led to the tentative identification . . . yes, anything you could add would be . . . fine . . . go ahead.'

O'Yee said into his phone, '. . . I don't know, Augusto . . . it all helps. Harry seems to think he's dead even though the general consensus of opinion seems to be that he's—' He listened for a while. 'Yeah, I saw it again about a month ago on the Late Movie. My favourite bit is when he says to Sam, "Play it, Sam." ' He said, one film cognisenti to another, 'He doesn't, does he? He never says, "Play it *again*, Sam," just "Play it, Sam." ' He laughed at something, 'Right. So what have you got?'

Feiffer said softly, 'Did he? . . . I really can't discuss it over the phone . . . I'd rather not say, Mr Weale . . . I appreciate it makes things simpler for you in relation to the partnership, but you have to appreciate that the investigation is still continuing. I'll let you know as soon as we do.' He found it difficult to hide the elation in his voice, 'Thank you very much for telling us.'

O'Yee said to Chagas, 'Enjoy the film.' He hung up as Feiffer did and looked over to see him smiling.

Feiffer said, 'That was Weale on the phone. He remembered something about Putnam. He said he didn't know whether it'd do any good or not, but he thought he'd mention it anyway.' He said, still smiling, 'Putnam once broke a bone in his ankle. Here, in Hong Kong.' He said triumphantly, 'He limped. Putnam did. The real Putnam. And so did the skeleton.' He nodded his head, 'Well, well, well . . .' He asked, 'Who was that?'

'Augusto Chagas in Macao.'

'And?'

'The teller remembered something else about the phoney Putnam.'

There was a silence. Feiffer looked at him with a feeling of terrible dread. 'What?'

O'Yee said hesitantly, 'The Putnam who picked up the money, the one whose description fits in every way, right down to the photo . . . . He said simply, 'He limped.'

He looked at Feiffer's face and thought that further elucidation was unnecessary.

11

It was 9 a.m. in the new day shift. The temperature in the
Detectives' Room was several degrees below freezing. During
the night someone of mechanical bent had taken a set of
spanners to the radiator and neatly and surgically, murdered
it. It lay, a victim of technological vivisection in a corner with
its innards out, the cat half asleep on its top dreaming of
warmth. O'Yee said for the second time in five minutes, trying
to concentrate his mind on things other than grief and
revenge, 'All you've got going for you on the ID are the teeth.
When you look at it objectively, everything points to the fact
that the man who picks up the money in Macao isn't an
impostor at all. He's the real Putnam.'

'Then who's in the grave? Someone he killed?'

'Possibly, yes. He could have planted the teeth there.'

'Working on the assumption that by putting his own set of
false teeth in with the body he'd remain anonymous?' Feiffer
said wearily, 'It doesn't figure. If he wanted to keep out of it
why bother? Why not use other teeth?'

Spencer said quietly, 'It's a bit hard to get teeth, Harry.'

'I know that! That's why I'm assuming they're either
Putnam's or the murderer's.'

'Harry, Putnam *is* the murderer!' O'Yee glanced at the
radiator and then decided to fix his mind on more wholesome
things. He looked at Auden, 'You haven't said anything. What
do you think?'

Auden rubbed at his chin thoughtfully.

O'Yee said, 'Great! What an incisive suggestion!' He

turned his attention to Feiffer, 'Look, the telex of the Army record only tells us that Putnam was an average sort of joe who looked like about ten million healthy young Americans at the time of the Korean war. The current passport photo shows an equally average looking middle-aged American with a full beard who could as well be Putnam as not. I just don't see why you're hanging onto the idea that the skeleton is Putnam. Everything militates against it.' He asked Spencer, 'Doesn't it?'

'Well, Christopher, I wouldn't like to be definite about it one way or the . . .'

Auden said suddenly, 'The more I think about it, the more sure I am that an elevator is a locked room. That means I solved a classic locked room mystery—did Sherlock Holmes ever have to solve a—'

O'Yee asked Feiffer, '*Why* can't the skeleton be someone else?'

'Because it just doesn't make any sense if it's someone else.'

'*Why* doesn't it?'

Feiffer paused for a moment. He was at his desk doodling something on a sheet of paper. Auden said to Spencer slowly, 'You know, the most famous locked room mystery was the one where this character had his head bashed in as he sat in an armchair reading a book. The room was locked from the inside and there were no windows and when the cops broke down the door there was no sign of a weapon. He was sitting under a light in a leather arm chair and there was no one else in the room . . .'

Spencer looked interested.

O'Yee's eyes fell irresistibly on the mutilated remains of his radiator. Something struck him. He asked Auden coldly, 'You didn't do this, did you?'

Feiffer said to the sheet of paper, 'If someone killed the real Putnam and then took his place why throw in the only piece of evidence that might suggest that Putnam was dead, namely his identifiable false teeth? You might as well have put a note in saying, "Putnam's dead. This is him. I'm taking his place. I'm an impostor." It doesn't make sense. If you wanted people to go on thinking he was alive why not destroy every form of identification? According to Kwok the teeth were found in the grave with the body, so either (1) they fell out and the murderer didn't think to take them away with him—which, in view of the way the so-called impostor has got just about everything right so far, is unlikely, or (2) he put them in with the body on purpose to make absolutely sure the identification was made. Which suggests that the teeth were the victims's, Putnam's—I mean, you don't have a pocket full of teeth with you on the off-chance you might just happen to kill someone and—'

Spencer said, 'The teeth couldn't have just fallen out and—?'

Auden said eagerly, 'He was killed by a block of dry ice hidden in the overhead light! It was fixed to fall on him when the heat from the light—' He plucked at Spencer's arm, 'And then it just evaporated!'

Feiffer said slowly, 'The fact that absolutely no traces of clothing were found suggests that the murderer stripped the corpse. That suggests he wasn't in a hurry. He took his time. I fail to see that he would have missed a complete set of false teeth. And Kwok claimed he found them on top of the body. No, the teeth were *put* there.' He asked the sheet of paper, 'The question is *why?*'

O'Yee said cautiously, 'Starting off from the theory that the skeleton is Putnam, what you've just proved is that it *isn't* Putnam.'

Auden said thoughtfully, 'It's a not totally dissimilar puzzle, this one . . .' He rubbed his chin to cogitate, 'To the celebrated Mystery of the—'

Spencer offered, 'If everything points to the fact that the Putnam who picks up the money in Macao is real, then who is the skeleton?' He asked, 'Harry, what makes you so sure that the Macao man is a phoney?'

Auden said cogitating, 'Good question.' He nodded at Spencer approvingly.

'What makes me think the Macao man is a phoney is that the Macao man is a phoney.' (Auden unseen by the others, looked baffled at that one.) 'If he's the real Putnam and everything is above board and he lives in Macao, then why the hell doesn't Chagas have any record of him? All right then, let's say he lives outside Macao and only comes in to collect his dough. Then, again, there should be some record of him coming and going. But there isn't any record of him coming and going. So, far from being the sort of legal Goody Two Shoes he pretends to be by paying his taxes and renewing his passport, either he lives in Macao or comes and goes in and out of it as someone else.' He said with an evil grin, 'And if he does that then he isn't Putnam. For the simple reason that Putnam is dead and has been for the last twenty years and he's the bastard who killed him!' He asked himself, 'But then why go to the trouble of setting evidence that the skeleton is Putnam? Why do that?'

Auden, nodding sagely, said 'When all the possible solutions have been exhausted then it must be the impossible that . . .'

O'Yee said to Feiffer, 'But then you're saying that whoever killed Putnam and left the teeth didn't give a damn whether he was identified or not. In other words, dead or alive, Putnam was just as useful to him.' He asked, 'What about his partner, Weale? He's in line to inherit, isn't he?'

'Weale's been paying out fifty per cent of his money for twenty years. I think if he'd killed Putnam he would have wanted the body found years ago. Putnam's no good to him alive. He's believed all these years that Putnam was still alive.'

O'Yee said desperately, 'Then maybe the man in Macao *is* Putnam!'

'Then why does he go to the trouble to hide his movements?'

'*I don't know!*'

Spencer said softly, 'I radio-pictured the fingerprints from the Army record to Captain Chagas the way you asked, Harry. He should have them this afternoon.'

'If he's got anything to compare them to.' Auden the quick-witted said, 'What about the bank slips? He must have had to fill out something to get the money.'

Feiffer said, 'And the bank must have filed it away. Or at least his original application for an account. Chagas could compare the Army prints with those. Right?'

'Right!'

Spencer said, 'Harry already thought of it. That's why I radio-pictured the prints over.'

'Well, I've been working on another case. I've just come to this one, haven't I?'

Spencer said, 'Oh, yes, Phil. I didn't mean that you . . .'

Feiffer said, 'It all helps. Thanks anyway, Phil.'

O'Yee asked, 'So what are the chances that the fingerprints will show it's the real Putnam?'

Feiffer said, 'Nil. The real Putnam is in Dawson Baume's mortuary.'

'You're sure of that aren't you?'

'No. I'm not sure of that!'

Spencer said, 'Why is it so important that the skeleton should be Putnam?'

O'Yee indicated Feiffer, 'Because he wants it to be Putnam.'

'I don't bloodywell want it to be Putnam!'

'You do. Something happened in that mortuary and now all you want to do is prove that it's George Edward—'

'The weight of evidence proves it's Putnam! And once we're absolutely certain that it is—'

O'Yee said, 'You intend to see someone go down for killing him.'

'Someone will go down for killing him.'

Auden asked, still rubbing his chin, 'And if it isn't Putnam?'

Feiffer ignored him. He asked Spencer, 'Do you know where the Hong Kong Immigrations Records Office is?'

'Yes, Harry. Why?'

'Because that's where you and Auden are going to be for the next few hours.'

'Doing what?' Auden said petulantly, 'You haven't answered my question.'

'What question was that?'

O'Yee watched Feiffer's face. He said quietly, 'You know very well what question that was. And the answer is that if the skeleton isn't Putnam we're never going to find out who it is. We're going to find out that the real Putnam is in Macao and as soon as we start sniffing around, going on past form, he's going to disappear again into thin air.' He said evenly, 'And you'll never know who the skeleton was.'

Feiffer said doggedly, 'It's Putnam.'

O'Yee nodded. He glanced at the radiator and then at Feiffer. He asked quietly, 'Is it?'

'Yes!'

O'Yee nodded. 'O.K. Sure.' He held up his hands in surrender, 'Whatever you say.'

He looked far from convinced.

TO . . . USEMBASSYHONGKONG . . . ATT. PASSPORT SECT.
FROM . . . DEPTDEFENCE WASHINGTON . . . STATUS . . .
UNCLASSIFIED . . . REQUESTED BY EMBASSYHONGKONG
AR/GEF/RGY 889

. . . EXTRACT ARMY RECORD . . . UNCLASSIFIED . . .
GEORGE EDWARD PUTNAM . . . DATE BIRTH APRIL SEVEN
1925 . . . NELSON ALABAMA USA . . . MALE CAUCASIAN
. . . PARENTS EDWARD R MARY K (BOTH DECEASED AUTO
ACCIDENT CALIFORNIA 1946) . . . DATE OF INDUCTION
AUGUST FIFTEEN 1951 . . . TRAINING MARYLAND USA . . .
UNITED NATIONS FORCES KOREAN POLICE ACTION . . .
DISCHARGED MAY SIX 1954 HONG KONG . . . HONORABLE
DISCHARGE . . . GOOD CONDUCT MEDAL . . . NO WOUNDS
OR DISABILITIES . . . RANK HELD AT DISCHARGE . . .
ACTING CORPORAL . . . DETAILS OF COMBAT SERVICE . . .
REAR AREA CLERK QUARTERMASTER'S SECTION . . .
COMMANDING OFFICER COMMENT . . . SATISFACTORY
SOLDIER . . . MILITARY POLICE COMMENT . . . NOTHING
KNOWN AGAINST THIS SOLDIER . . .
HEIGHT . . . FIVE FOOT ELEVEN ONE QUARTER INCHES . . .

BUILD . . . MEDIUM . . . WEIGHT ONE SIXTY THREE
POUNDS . . .
EYES . . . BROWN . . .
HAIR . . . BROWN . . .
SPECIAL FEATURES . . . NONE . . .
MEDICAL HISTORY . . . MILD SINUSITIS CONDITION . . .
VISION 20-20 . . . HEARING 96% . . . PSYCHOLOGICAL
TESTING IQ . . . AVERAGE . . . BLOOD PRESSURE ETC . . .
NORMAL . . . ALLERGIES . . . ANIMAL FUR HAY FEVER . . .
(SINUSITIC CONDITION) . . . COMMUNICABLE OR HEREDI-
TARY DEFECTS OR DISEASES . . . NONE . . . CHILDHOOD
APPENDECTOMY SCAR . . . MEDICAL RATING AT TIME OF
DISCHARGE . . . SATISFACTORY . . .
PHOTOGRAPH . . . TO FOLLOW . . .
FINGERPRINTS . . . TO FOLLOW . . .
MARITAL STATUS AT DISCHARGE . . . SINGLE . . .
NEXT OF KIN . . . NONE . . .
LAST KNOWN ADDRESS . . . P.O. BOX NUMBER HONG KONG
. . . BELIEVED PRESENTLY HONG KONG RESIDENT . . .
SECURITY RATING . . . SATISFACTORY . . .
ACCESS TO CONFIDENTIAL OR CLASSIFIED DOCUMENTS
DURING SERVICE . . . NONE . . .
SPECIAL SKILLS . . . TYPING . . .
SMALL ARMS QUALIFICATIONS . . . GARAND RIFLE . . . MI
CARBINE . . .
RATING . . . AVERAGE . . .
NO FURTHER INFORMATION . . . NO FURTHER INFOR-
MATION . . .
FOLLOWUPS TO MESSAGE . . . PHOTOGRAPH AND FINGER-
PRINTS . . . DESPATCHED SIMULTANEOUSLY TO
USEMBASSYHONGKONG . . .
MESSAGE ENDS . . . END UNCLASSIFIED RATING . . . RESET
RATING . . .
MESSAGE ENDS . . .

O'Yee said, 'So he's a cipher.' He picked up the reproduction photograph and considered it for a moment, 'He could be anyone. He looks like your typical picture of Mr Klean with a GI haircut and pimples on his face. I'm not surprised he grew a beard.' He ran his finger down the telex and stopped at the combat record, 'A clerk typist . . .' He passed the paper over to Feiffer and said as a comment on George Edward Putnam, the finding of a skeleton washed up on a beach twenty years later, people lurking about collecting money on the strength of passports that entitled them to go anywhere that they evidently used to go nowhere, the American Army, the sleeping cat, the dismembered radiator, Feiffer, and the world in general: 'Terrific.'

In the dusty vaults of the Hong Kong Immigration Records Room, The Great Detective paused and searched the face of his assistant for revelation. The face of his assistant was down over a desk laden with boxes of dusty records and there was no revelation to be had. The Great Detective said, 'We're wasting our time.' He had a similar mountain of records on his own desk and he pushed them to one side and pondered.

Auden The Great said slowly, 'It is patently obvious to me that if he was in Hong Kong and he went to Macao without anyone at Macao Immigration noticing, then he left here and came back again without anyone in Hong Kong noticing either.' A deduction. 'In my opinion, we are wasting valuable time.' A conclusion. 'I come to Harry Feiffer's view that the real Putnam is lying dead in the Mortuary.'

Spencer turned over another banded hundred immigration cards and began flipping through them.

'You have to understand the criminal mind.' Auden shoved his own cards farther away. He shoved the cards away yet again. 'All this grubbing through files is a waste of time. I ask you: who got Ong the mugger?'

Spencer said, 'You did, Phil.'

'I did. And I didn't defeat him by grubbing through cards, I defeated him by logic.' He said thoughtfully, 'There's a single weak link in all this and we must bring our minds to bear on it and uncover it.' He thought it was probably a One Cigarette Problem. He lit the cigarette slowly and drew on it. The exhaled smoke curled fug-like around his head. 'Consider the skeleton from both angles simultaneously: one, that it *is* Putnam and two, that it isn't . . .'

Spencer leaned back in his chair and listened.

'Now—try to follow this closely—now, if it's the real Putnam who's in Macao collecting his money with his own passport then the skeleton in the water couldn't have been him. Right?'

'Right.'

'Right. O.K.' He drew in on the cigarette preparatory to unleashing the mighty brain for a second foray into the world of the conundrum, 'And if the person in Macao who says he's Putnam *isn't Putnam* then it's a fair guess that, because he has all the documents and so on, that he *killed* the real Putnam and the real Putnam is the skeleton.' He paused, lost himself for a moment, 'So Putnam is the skeleton, right?'

Spencer nodded carefully.

'Now, we know that the person isn't getting in and out of Macao using Putnam's passport. Whether or not he leaves Hong Kong on it is beside the point—' (he waved his hand at the cards to reiterate the time-wasting conviction) 'The point is that he doesn't get into Macao as Putnam. So why not?'

Spencer said, 'Because the real Putnam is dead?'

'Right. And he planted the false teeth on the real Putnam to throw suspicion off himself.'

'But if the skeleton is Putnam they're Putnam's teeth.'

Auden coughed at his cigarette, 'Right! I was hoping you'd pick that one up!' He said quickly, 'Of course he didn't plant them. He just *found* them when he killed Putnam and put them in the grave with him to *hide* them.'

'But don't you think he would have known we'd find the body sooner or later?'

'That's why he stripped the clothes off it.'

'Then why leave the teeth?'

Auden paused. He thought that one through. He said thoughtfully, 'Hmm . . .'

Spencer said softly, 'According to all the descriptions, the man in Macao *is* Putnam. I tend to agree with Christoper O'Yee that the skeleton is someone else.'

'Who?'

'Someone Putnam killed and tried to disguise as himself.'

Auden said quickly, 'Right. In order to make himself into someone else.'

Spencer asked, 'Then why does he pick the money up as Putnam?'

'Because that's the motive for the whole crime! So simple, so easy.'

Spencer said, 'So the murderer can pretend he's Putnam? You just told me that he *is* Putnam.'

'No! I was just proving that he wasn't.'

'But you just proved that he was.'

'No, I didn't!'

Spencer said mildly, 'You did actually, Phil.'

'Did I?'

'Yes . . .'

Auden paused. Time to evaluate another line of reasoning. 'The motive was the money in Macao.' He looked at Spencer expectantly.

'Well, nothing else has come to light so far.'

'All right, then *so far* the motive is the money in Macao!'

'Well, it is so far, isn't it . . . ?'

'Shut up!' The Great Mind was getting a little rattled.

Auden said, 'So . . .' He pulled on the cigarette and cleared the celebrated cerebellum with nicotine wash, 'So if the murderer wasn't Putnam, he killed Putnam and took his place so he could collect the money. Right?'

'Then why did he . . .'

'*Right*? Just wait will you! And he got hold of Putnam's passport and faked it—right?'

'The photographs wouldn't match.'

'One passport photograph looks the same as another,

132

doesn't it?' (Spencer started to shake his head) 'Anyway, he had a beard didn't he?'

'Well, yes . . .'

'And then he simply went across to Macao using his own passport and presented Putnam's at the bank and collected his money. Simple. So the skeleton in the grave was the real Putnam. Right. Simple? Right!'

'Then why didn't he take the teeth when he stripped the body?'

'Maybe he bloodywell forgot them: how do I know?'

'He put them on top of the skeleton's chest to be found. So when the skeleton was found we'd think it was Putnam.'

Auden said, 'It is Putnam. I've just proved it.'

'Then why would he go to the trouble of doing it? Why not just leave Putnam's identification and make it easier in the first place?' Spencer asked, 'And if he was taking Putnam's place and collecting his money, why ever would he want us to think Putnam was dead? Surely that'd be the end of everything for him?' He shook his head, 'No, whoever killed that man didn't care whether we thought it was Putnam or not.'

'Right!' Auden said, 'And that's why he stripped the body!'

'Why?'

'Well . . . because of what I've just led you to say . . .'

Spencer said, 'But you haven't led me to say anything. All I said was that the killer didn't care what we thought one way or the other. But he cared enough about something to strip the body.'

'He didn't care if we identified Putnam through the teeth, but he did care whether or not we identified him through his documents.' Auden said as to a cretinous simpleton, 'You see, by leaving the teeth he wanted us to think that the body was Putnam. You see?'

'I thought you said you'd come round to Harry Feiffer's view that the skeleton *was* Putnam?' He looked at Auden's face, 'Phil?'

133

Auden said nothing. The cigarette burned away of its own accord in his mouth.

Spencer said helpfully, 'I'm sure if we went on, I'm sure you'll come up with the right solution . . .' He flipped a few cards in his hand in case it was the Singular Mind's final conclusion that the answer lay in the cards. (With an Investigator like Auden you could never tell whether or not he was just testing you.) After all, the locked elevator mystery, compared to his own humble performance at P. P. Fan's . . . Spencer thought a good detective could always learn from the methods of others: He waited.

Auden looked at him.

Spencer smiled encouragingly. He leaned forward, all attention.

Auden said, 'This fellow Putnam . . .'

'Yes?'

There was a faint twitch under Auden's left eye, 'In my opinion . . . this fucking bastard Putnam—'

Spencer said excitedly, 'Yes—?'

Auden shouted, 'He doesn't fucking *exist*!'

He went back to his files.

Chagas' voice said urgently over the telephone, 'Harry, something's come up. There was something just a bit funny about the teller at the bank trying to be so helpful when he hadn't seen that fellow Putnam for so long, so I went back to the bank and had a few words to him in English. And all that stuff about him being the only one who could understand Putnam's mint julep accent is just so much eyewash. His English stinks. What made him remember Putnam was that he did him a little favour and made a few dollars out of it: he supplied him with a bit of female companionship. What do you think of that?'

Feiffer put his hand over the mouthpiece of the telephone and looked over at O'Yee. He took his hand away and asked Chagas, 'What's her name?'

'Ah . . .'

'What do you mean, "ah"?'

Chagas said in a disgusted whisper, 'God, these European names Chinese girls pick! Her name's Pansy Yi.'

'Is she still in Macao?'

'That's the "ah". We don't know. Neither does the moon-lighting pimp bank teller. At least he says he doesn't. So far it's all just been him and me having quiet little chats at the teller's cage. If I turn up and demand the whereabouts of this girl brandishing notebooks, I'm afraid I may discover that the bank teller doesn't know what I'm talking about and that Pansy Yi and the whole thing may just disappear into a combination of job-protecting and protesting bank managers.' He said to add a little weight to the assertion, 'The Macao police don't mind doing small favours for their Hong Kong counterparts, but if you want the full bugle-blowing it'll have to be cleared through your senior officer.' He asked, 'Do you happen to be on those sort of good terms with your Commander at the moment?'

Feiffer said nothing.

'I see.' Chagas made a clucking noise with his tongue. 'I'm still not even certain what it is you want me to find out here. This man who collects the money isn't the man he claims to be, is that correct?'

'I think so.'

'Well, is he or isn't he?'

'I don't know. We've got a body and we—I—think it's. an American named Putnam. Therefore, I'm inclined to think that your Putnam in Macao is a fake.' He said urgently, 'Surely the fact that we can't find any record of him would mean that—'

'All that would mean, Harry, officially, is that maybe there's been a slip-up at Immigration. I can't go into a Macao bank waving my arms around with nothing more than that.' He paused for a moment, 'I can see what the teller might volunteer, but you appreciate I have to have something stronger to threaten him with than that. And if I say that it could be a bank fraud I might scare him completely.'

Feiffer said lamely, 'What would Louis Renault do?'

'Louis Renault would fade off into the distance with Ingrid Bergman.' Chagas said very seriously, 'I don't mind doing you the odd favour, Harry, but messing around with banks in a free port like Macao is a sure recipe for getting your balls caught in a mincer.'

'Then forget the bank fraud bit.'

'And replace it with what?'

'With the murder.'

'Yes, Harry, but what murder?' Chagas drew a breath, 'I don't want to extract confidential information out of you—I understand that at this stage you might be still a bit in the dark yourself, but I have to at least have a good grip on one aspect of it, and it's this: this fellow Putnam, is he dead or not?'

'I don't know.'

'Well, you must know!'

'Well, I bloodywell don't!' Feiffer thought for an instant of the shape under the white sheet, of bumping into it and saying without thinking . . . He said desperately into the phone, 'Augusto, I don't know if he's dead or not. Someone is.' He put his free hand to his forehead and said softly, 'God Almighty . . .'

There was a long silence from the Macao end and then Chagas' voice said softly, 'O.K.'

'I'm sorry, Augusto, I just don't know what to . . .'

'All right.' Chagas said in a kindly tone, 'All right, I'll see what I can do.'

The line went dead as, in his office on the Avenida de Sidonio Pais overlooking the wide still streets of the oldest colony in Asia, Chagas carefully replaced the receiver.

12

The extension number inside the American Embassy rang and rang and rang. If there was somebody at the number—whereever it was deep inside the bowels of the place—then he was waiting a very long time before deciding to pick it up. It was the third time O'Yee had been transferred to another section: he was getting tired of it. He watched the cat sleeping on top of the radiator and—

The extension stopped ringing. There was another long pause and then a deep voice said very reluctantly, 'Herxheimer.'

O'Yee said, 'Mr—?'

The long pause again. The voice said in a completely flat tone, 'Herxheimer.'

'Mr Herxheimer?'

The voice said nothing. In the background there was absolutely no sound at all.

O'Yee said, 'Senior Detective Inspector O'Yee, Hong Kong Police.'

Nothing.

'The Embassy switchboard connected me with you. I've been trying to get some information about an American citizen issued a passport at the Embassy—'

It was like talking to a fish.

'—And they put me on to you—'

Herxheimer said evenly, 'How did you get my name?'

'You just gave it to me.'

'Before.'

'The switchboard connected me.' There was another long silence. For an instant O'Yee thought he heard the sound of a teleprinting machine, then a heavy soundproof door seemed to be closed and it was gone again.

Herxheimer said, 'And you claim to be an officer in the Hong Kong police.' It was not a question. He paused again and added without threat or rancour, 'This call is being traced to its source. So you had better be ringing from a police station.'

'Mr Herxheimer, which section of the Embassy do you represent?' There was absolutely no reply. O'Yee said, 'Oh. That one.'

Herxheimer said flatly, 'You're an American.'

'Chinese-American.'

'Why are you working for a foreign government?'

'Pardon?'

'If you're an American why are you working in the pay of a foreign government?'

'The British Crown Colony of Hong Kong is hardly a foreign government.'

Herxheimer said, unconvinced, 'Oh?' He paused, 'Have you formally and finally renounced U.S. citizenship according to law?'

'No, I haven't formally and finally renounced U.S. citizenship. I also haven't renounced Hong Kong residence. As a matter of fact, I've got State Department permission to be employed by—' O'Yee demanded suddenly, 'Why the hell are you asking all the questions? I'm the one who wants to ask questions, not you!'

'What sort of Chinese name is O'Yee?'

'It's a Chinese-Irish name, if you really want to know!'

'I thought you said you were Chinese-*American*?'

'I'm Chinese-*Irish*-American—all right?'

Herxheimer said softly, 'Chinese-Irish-*Amer*—?'

'What sort of fucking name is *Herxheimer*?'

'It's an American name.'

O'Yee glanced at the cat: 'Listen, Herxheimer, or what-ever your name is—'

Herxheimer said with perfect even temper, 'It's Herx-heimer.'

'Well, if you've now had the call traced, my name and history run through the computer, and the whole schtick written in invisible ink in your secret agent's little black book, do you think we can put Joe McCarthy back in his cupboard for a few seconds and get on with some *answers*?'

'Like what?'

'Like George Edward Putnam!'

Herxheimer said nothing.

'You've had a routine report about him. Haven't you? I mean, you do get things like that, don't you? Down there in Spook-Land? You do get all—don't you?' There was still, eternally, no reply. 'God, you haven't the faintest idea what I'm talking about, have you?'

'Tell me again.'

O'Yee said patiently, 'George Edward Putnam. We requested his Army record from Washington. I thought you people in Snoopsville knew everything about everything—'

Herxheimer said warningly, 'I hope you realise everything you say is being recorded.'

O'Yee ignored him. 'We have reason to believe that the U.S. passport issued to him—in fact a number of passports issued to him over the last twenty years—have been used for illegal purposes.' He imagined Herxheimer as a big, humour-less bugger with a thin tie—'In fact they haven't been used for the purpose for which they were issued at all.'

'Which is?'

O'Yee said with heavy condescension, 'Travel. We have reason to believe Putnam is entering and leaving Macao and Hong Kong using false papers.'

'And?'

O'Yee said, 'And we can't locate him. We want you people to get onto the U.S. Immigration Service and the local police and find out his present whereabouts in the United States.'

'Is that where he is? In the United States?'

'We don't know where he is!'

'Then what makes you think he's there?'

'*Because, to the best of our knowledge, he sure as hell isn't over here!*'

'Should he be?'

'He should be in Macao!'

'Then ask the Macao police.'

'We have asked the Macao police! There's no record of him.'

'Then how do you know he was ever there?'

O'Yee drew a deep breath. 'Because he's been *seen* there. O.K?' O'Yee said, shaking his head, 'It beats me why they put me onto you.'

'They put you onto me because I'm in charge of the investigation.'

'*What* investigation?'

'The investigation into the current location of George Edward Putnam, U.S. citizen.' Herxheimer said quietly, 'I can tell you that no one using that name has presented himself at an American port of entry in the last twenty-five years.' He paused, 'When was the last time he was seen in Hong Kong?'

'Twenty-plus years ago.'

'Following the Korean War.'

'Well, yes, I suppose so.'

'And then in Macao.' Herxheimer said, 'The question is, how does he enter Macao without using his passport, is that it?'

'Up to a point, yes.'

Herxheimer said, 'Hmm.'

'Well, can you help us?'

'I have helped you. I've told you he isn't in the United States.' He asked easily, without changing tone, 'Do you go back to your own country regularly, Mr O'Yee? Or do you stay here in a foreign state full-time?'

'I'm not under bloody investigation—Putnam is!'

'I don't see why a good American should mind another

American asking him when he last went back home.' Herxheimer asked ominously, 'You do consider the United States
of America your home?' He put a very large question mark at
the end of the sentence.

O'Yee said nothing.

Without uttering a syllable, Herxheimer made an even
larger question mark.

O'Yee said, 'It's been nice talking to you, whoever you are,
and I hope you have a very satisfying day playing with your
thumbscrews.'

Herxheimer made a grunting noise.

O'Yee said maliciously, 'What was that?'

Herxheimer's deep, flat voice suggested without emotion,
'There are basically only three ways to get in or out of any
country.' He paused again. (O'Yee had a picture of him
laboriously counting out the ways on his fingers.) 'One, to fly
in or out on an aircraft—'

'You can't fly in or out of Macao on an aircraft. There's no
airport.'

'To come or leave by ship—in the case of Macao without
a deep water harbour, by ferry or hydrofoil . . .'

'Which we've checked and which is why I'm ringing
you.'

'And, overland.' Herxheimer said, 'You'll keep me in the
picture?' He paused. 'We're always interested in this department when one of our citizens goes missing. Particularly in
this part of the world . . .' He paused as the sound of the
teleprinter came on as background noise and then stopped as
the soundproof door was closed tight, 'You've got my
number?'

'I've got your name.'

'Which name is that?'

'*Herxheimer!*'

'Oh yeah.' Herxheimer—or whoever it was—said cheerfully,
'Just keep in touch.' He dropped his voice, 'And Mr O'Yee—'

'What?'

'Oh . . . nothing . . .'

There was a click as the tape recorder was turned off a few seconds before he hung up.

O'Yee stared at the cat. Feiffer was at his desk re-reading the photostat of the Army record for the umpteenth ime. O'Yee said, 'You can't fly into Macao, can you?'

Feiffer shook his head.

'And there isn't a deep water port there?'

'No. You know that. Why are you asking me things you already know?'

'I don't know. I was just thinking about—' He thought, *"Overland?"* How the hell did you come into Macao overland? Macao was connected by a single narrow isthmus to nothing but— 'The only place overland from Macao is—' He said, 'Oh my God, Communist China!'

Feiffer said wearily, 'Goodness, but you're a clever lad. Take a gold star for geography.' He looked at O'Yee's face and then back down to the Army records. He said casually, 'Forget it.'

O'Yee said, 'Yeah.' He nodded. Herxheimer . . . O'Yee said in his strongest American accent, 'Damn right. Forget it!' He nodded to himself and tried to think of something stronger. He said, 'Right on!'

Feiffer said without looking up, 'Do me a favour and shut up, will you?'

O'Yee nodded.

Herxheimer . . .

O'Yee said softly to himself, 'As American as . . .' He paused. If there was one thing Chinese families in America never, never ate it was . . .

He thought to himself, "I'm as American as . . ."

Peking duck and noodles . . . ?

Chagas' voice said dismally on the telephone, 'Harry? We've got her, the elusive Miss Pansy Yi, and she is not saying a single solitary word. Not one measly syllable.'

'What, nothing at all?'

'Less than nothing. Two mathematical points below minus

zero.' He dropped his voice, 'And because of you and it, old pal, your one-time Macao colleague, Captain Augusto Carlos Chagas, late of the Portuguese Colonial et cetera and so on, is very fast disappearing in the general direction of the nearest garbage disposal site.'

'What's happening?'

'From Miss Pansy Yi, nothing is happening. From the rest of Macao, the world is fast falling down around my ears. I warned you about this.' He lowered his voice yet again, 'Miss Pansy Yi is an employed working girl. Miss Pansy Yi's employers are the local secret society. Not your harmless murdering gang of Hong Kong type thugs, the 14-K, but the real, fully blown, politically oriented Macao variety who, to the best of my knowledge, don't even have a name.' He asked rhetorically, 'If you rule the world, why bother calling yourself anything but the rulers of the world?' He said with a tremor in his voice, 'And presently, the rulers of the world are not happy. And guess who they're not happy with?' He went on before Feiffer could interrupt, 'Oh, and that's not all. The bank now seems to have a fair idea that I, Augusto Carlos Chagas, the soon to be shot, knifed, bashed or otherwise pulped, have been sniffing around illegally trying to cajole information about an account from one of their clerks. They haven't bothered to report the fact to my boss, thank God, and ask if I've got official blessing, because they know in the first place I wouldn't have *got* official blessing!'

'I'm sorry about this, Augusto—'

Chagas said very carefully and patiently, like a man dictating his will, 'Oh, it gets far worse. You see, Miss Pansy Yi is employed and protected by the secret society because the secret society runs the world around here. Except, ah-ha, for the little matter of the six hundred million Communists just across the road in China. Ho-ho, too easy: the secret society has come to an arrangement with the Communists that, in return for the secret society supporting the Communists at the occasional bloody riot we have here in Macao every five or six years and on alternate Wednesdays, the Communists

143

support the secret society. We cops, nobody supports us.' His voice hardened, 'And, as a consequence, Miss Pansy Yi, nubile long stemmed sylph that she is, is sitting next door in my office drinking tea and wondering whether or not she should ring up the entire People's Red Army and have them come down here to cut my heart out!' He said in a whisper, 'I'm ringing from a public call box in the corridor. *And that's probably bugged!*'

'She didn't tell you anything at all about Putnam?'

'*No, Harry, she didn't tell me anything at all about Putnam!*' He asked, 'Do I sound hysterical? Good. That's what I am.'

'She must know something about him.'

'Why do you keep asking about Putnam? What about me?'

'I can't believe it's as bad as you—'

'YOU CAN'T BELIEVE WHAT?'

Feiffer said, 'What can we do to help?'

'What you can do to help is get me off the chopping block! I can see myself back in Lisbon in about thirty-five seconds trying to explain why the hell I alone, after three hundred years of patient trade and administration, in one fell swoop managed to lose the entire colony of—' He said in a rising tone of desperation, 'Macao is one of the oldest colonies in the world! I'll be back home in Portugal pressing grapes with my *nose!*'

'Is there any way of putting some pressure on her?'

'Are you serious? I thought she was just some little bank clerk's girlfriend picking up a few dollars on the side. She's under the protection of half the armed might on the continent of Asia! Yes, I can put some pressure on her. I can get down on my knees and make an act of contrition to her, or I can open a vein and let her use my blood for hair dye or I can—all I want from that girl at the moment is one thing: a free pardon!'

'Wait a minute—'

'I haven't got a minute.' Chagas said miserably, 'Oh, you've done it to me this time . . .'

'Maybe we could bring some influence to bear on her from this end—'

'That I'd like to see. The colonial British Empire what's left of it sailing a gunboat into the Praya Grande and lobbing a few shells onto—have you got any influence in Peking? No? Canton? Shanghai?' He said maliciously, 'Hong Kong? Know any powerful Communists who owe you a favour?'

Feiffer paused. He said quietly, 'As a matter of fact, Augusto, I do.'

'*Really?*'

'Really.'

Chagas said, 'Honest?' He made a swallowing sound at the other end of the line. 'Harry, this could be the beginning of a beautiful . . .' The words stuck in his throat.

'But I still want your local whore to—'

'Don't say that!'

'—to come up with a bit of information.'

Chagas said in the background in Chinese to what Feiffer assumed was a passing cleaner or traffic policeman, 'Just ringing the wife, you know—ha . . .' He said desperately, 'Anything. O.K? Anything.' He said in a harsh whisper, 'Harry?'

'Yes?'

'Just hurry, will you?'

He replaced the receiver and, in the corridor, plucked at the epaulettes and gold braid on his shoulders nervously.

Feiffer said sweetly, 'Phil—! How are you?' (Auden looked around in the Detectives' Room to see if someone else named Phil had come in behind him.) 'Any luck with that dreary task I sent you on?'

'No.'

Feiffer looked at Spencer. Spencer said pleasantly, 'Hullo, boss.'

Feiffer ignored him. 'I've been thinking about your theories, Phil, and by God, I'm sure you've got more than a grain of truth in them—'

O'Yee said in concert, 'Several grains. A lot of grains.' He had one hand on the telephone ready to dial a number.

Auden said, 'Oh? Really?'

'Really, Phil.' Feiffer bunched his fist and made a decisive blow in the general direction of all the conundrums of the world, 'A man like you—'

Auden said, 'Yeah . . .' He looked at Spencer and winked at him conspiratorially.

Feiffer said casually, 'Phil, about this character Ong you picked up—you know, the one with the cousin who's a big shot in the Communist set-up around here . . .'

Auden said suspiciously, 'I'm not opposing bail.'

'Now, Phil . . .'

'I've got him scared, Harry, I don't need to oppose bail.' He saw Feiffer's face and O'Yee's hand poised above the telephone. He said in a voice that carried with it the coming rags of defeat, 'Oh, no, Harry . . .'

Feiffer said reasonably, 'Now, Phil, far be it from me to pull rank on you . . .'

Auden said like a little boy, 'Aw, gee, Harry . . .'

His associate, subordinate and chronicler, Watson looked away.

13

Chagas' voice said happily over the line, 'She's burbling away like a bird, Harry. Everything.'

'You're off the hook?'

'Am I off the hook! Right now I'm the policeman most likely to be presented to the Pope! Everyone loves me: Pansy Yi loves me so much she can't wait to unburden her burdened little black heart, the bank loves me—I'm preventing a fraud perpetrated against them by some evil, conniving European villain—' (He said in an undertone, 'I discover the secret society keeps their funds there') '—the Communists have decided with a man like me at the helm the colony is in good hands for another fifty years, and my boss has just rung up and said in a kindly voice, "Augusto, my dear friend, what's this I hear about you bringing the opposing factions in Macao into happy harmony?"' He asked, still dazed, 'What did you do?'

'Just the usual combination of tact, diplomacy and brilliance.' Feiffer asked evenly, 'What has she been saying?'

'The curvaceous Pansy? Quite a lot. It turns out, did you know, that she's just a poor, good-hearted girl who has a widowed mother and three younger brothers and sisters to support and that really she would have co-operated with the police in the first place only she was tearfully afraid that because she fell from the path of virtue once or twice it might get around that she wasn't a nice girl.' He paused, out of breath. 'And she's engaged, did you know, to a poor hard-working farmer who, with his own hands, is busily, even at this moment, building their little dream house from the very clay of the earth—' He made a snuffling noise, 'Heartbreaking, isn't it? And she is beaten, yes beaten, twice or three times a day by the cruel man who has forced her into a life of vice.' He said quietly, 'She even offered to show me her scars at a reduced rate.' He paused for a moment, 'Putnam—'

'Putnam—'

'Ah, Putnam. Evidently the first and last time she saw him was about five or six months ago. Does that tally with what you know?'

'It tallies. And she still remembers him?'

'I thought that was strange too. But, she says, she's only fallen once or twice from the paths of— But she does remember him. He was one of her odder customers. There's also the fact that, so far as I can determine, she normally works out of one of the secret society fronts and almost all her customers are Chinese society men or their hangers-on. Evidently, the bank teller is an independent, a part-timer, and Putnam's the only European he ever sent to her. Although I still couldn't see how that might engrave him indelibly in her mind . . .'

Feiffer asked, 'Does the description fit?'

'It does, yes.'

'Down to the limp?'

'Ah, the limp. The limp, she says, rather comes and goes. It's more an odd walk.'

Feiffer smiled to himself.

Chagas said softly, 'After a session with the athletic Pansy I could see why anyone might walk oddly . . .'

'If she picked him up at the bank he was walking oddly *before* he had his session.'

'Sure. In any event, no session took place. That's another reason she remembers him.' He added, 'And what might just keep her from getting herself beaten to a frazzle by her right-eously offended employer. According to her, this fellow Putnam went to her room with her (no quick pokes against a wall for him) and spent the entire afternoon sitting in the dark looking at his watch. According to Pansy the Earth

Mother, she thought he might have been a queer on the verge of taking the cure.' He said in parenthesis, 'I'll spare you the graphic details of Pansy's cure for the limp-wristed—but no, evidently he told her to fuck off in very strong heterosexual tones and continued to sit there looking at his watch.'

'What was he waiting for? Any idea?'

'The ferry.'

'Back to Hong Kong?'

'Back to Hong Kong. The overnight ferry. The one with private cabins. This fellow didn't want to be seen. Approximately fifty minutes before it was due to leave, he sent Pansy out.'

'In order to do what?'

'Ah-ha. That's the question. In order to have privacy for something. The understanding Pansy however, not being a girl to be easily put off, hung around in the street and watched him as he came out.'

'Limp?'

Chagas said, 'No limp. It was dark, so she only saw his silhouette, but there was no limp.'

'I knew it was Putnam!'

'What?'

'I knew Putnam was dead . . .'

'Oh. Well, if your friend Putnam was a limper then Pansy's friend wasn't Putnam. There's more. It's a little bit odd, this part, but you can have it for what it's worth: Pansy, whose English really isn't so good, but whose body language is well above the pass rate, informed me (crinkling up her small empty head) that although this fellow was about fifty or so—' He asked in parenthesis, 'Would that be about the right age for Putnam?'

'Yes.'

'—that although he was about fifty or so, he—' He hesitated, 'This sounds a bit silly—'

Feiffer said urgently, 'Go on.'

'Well, he behaved as if he was only in his twenties. The word she used was "boyish". I suppose she ought to know.

149

Can you make anything of that? He more or less ebbed and flowed as first a man in his fifties and then, bingo! he was moving around like some young kid—sort of gangly and—' He said, a little embarrassed, 'Does that make any sense or is Pansy just gilding the lily?'

'It makes sense.'

'How?'

'The real Putnam was killed when he was about twenty nine or thirty. If this character was impersonating him the way he remembered him—'

'Oh. I see. So the killer must have known him?'

'I would have thought that was a hundred percent certainty.'

Chagas offered, 'And if he's been impersonating him all those years I suppose the characterisation hasn't grown up— Fascinating. I ought to send Pansy along to lecture on identification techniques at the police academy.' He added, 'By the way, did I mention the bank sent along a pile of withdrawal and demand slips from Putnam's transactions? They've all been filed away, untouched by other hands, for almost twenty years, some of them. They sent them around via a messenger wearing white gloves with the slips wrapped up in a cellophane bag. I've passed them on to Scientific so they can compare them with the Army prints you sent me, and you should have the good news by this afternoon.' He asked, 'Is there anything else the Hero of the East can do for you?'

'The man who picks up the money isn't Putnam.'

'I'd say that was a more than reasonable assumption at this point, yes.'

'Then in that case you've done everything for me you possibly could.' Feiffer said good-humouredly, 'Unless you're holding the clincher up your sleeve.'

'Don't I always?'

'Invariably.' Feiffer said, 'What is it? Did the erstwhile Pansy give him a knock-out drop or something and go through his pockets? And bingo! you know his real name.' He asked hopefully, 'Right?'

'Wrong. Pansy is a nice girl.' He paused for a moment, 'No, what Pansy, the wellspring of varied experience, did was to smell something.'

Feiffer said wearily, 'I hate to think what you're going to say . . .'

'Tut-tut. Pansy, lady of much learning and human perception once worked in an emporium of the performing arts—I believe it was called in translation, "The Naked Pussy"—not quite where you might find Sir Laurence Olivier and Dame Edith Evans treading the boards, but still—and there, mingling as she did with some of the male actors whose brief (and I mean brief) representation of a traditional fourteenth century Chinese opera preceded for the sake of the licence the main attraction, *Strippers With Whips*, Pansy first made acquaintance with the smell she smelled in Putnam's presence.' He waited for full dramatic effect. 'I must say, by the way, that I missed *Strippers With Whips* . . .'

'What was it?'

'Spirit gum.'

'What?'

'Spirit gum. Kryolan Number Four. He smelled of it.'

'I don't understand.'

Chagas made a muted chortling noise. 'You have to be up close to smell it. At one stage, she got up close. (The attempted patent queer cure.) Gum Arabic. A great job, Pansy informed me professionally, almost perfect, near to the summit of technique, except for the smell.' He paused again, 'And then, when she saw him in the street, it was gone. That and the limp. That was why he sent her out early. He had to remove it before he went down to the ferry and came back to Hong Kong as someone else—' Chagas said, 'I've got your description of the real Putnam in front of me: the one from the passport application: medium build, brown hair, brown eyes, beard, the lot.' He went on quickly, 'The *beard*, Harry, spirit gum, Kryolan Number Four.' He said in triumph, 'The *beard*— It was false. He removed it when he sent her out. And before you ask, cabin bookings for ferries are sold on a first-come basis, so we can't check who he really was, but that beard was false, and I can tell you one thing: whoever it was who picked up that money at the bank . . .'

Feiffer said, 'It sure as hell wasn't Putnam.'

Feiffer said definitively into the telephone, 'Putnam's dead.'

'Is that for sure?' Weale's voice had an edge to it. He seemed to be having a hard time keeping his enthusiasm down, 'I mean, that's really for sure? That bastard is really—dead?'

'Yes.'

'My God, that's wonderful!'

'It has to be confirmed one hundred percent from Macao this afternoon, but as far as the police are concerned, Putnam is lying in the Hong Bay mortuary waiting to be claimed.'

'Christ! That's—' Weale said, 'That's—' He made an enormous sigh of relief, 'God, I can't tell you how long he's been—and it wasn't even him! Christ, it was some other bastard bleeding me! Have you got him yet?'

'Enquiries are proceeding.'

'But it's as sure as shit that Eddie's dead?'

'It's almost certain.'

'Almost?'

Feiffer said, 'It's certain. In due course the coroner's inquest can go ahead and then he can be buried.'

Weale said enthusiastically, 'I'll pay for it! Christ, all these years and I thought it was Eddie bleeding me—and the poor mother's been dead for—I'll pay for the funeral! All the things I've thought about that—and it was some other lousy s.o.b. all these years!' He paused for a moment and went on in a puzzled tone, 'I thought there was nothing much in the world that could surprise me, but Jesus, that's surprised me—it was someone else . . .' He said exuberantly, 'Mr Feiffer, if ever you're in the vicinity of *The Crap Game* and you feel like drinking the house dry, don't bring any money!'

'Thanks.'

'I mean it. Christ!' He hesitated. His voice dropped thoughtfully, 'I'll have to consider this now. With—with a lawyer. I've been paying for—' He said suddenly, 'Whoever was collecting the dough must have been the one who killed him—right?'

'It's likely.'

'And you'll get him.'

'Maybe.'

'You will. Christ, if anyone can get him you guys will. Can I do anything?'

'You can pay the next instalment to Macao.'

'Are you off your rocker?' He halted, 'Yeah, right! And when this other guy turns up to collect it, you—but when the hell are you going to—the next payment isn't until June next year—what about Eddie?'

'I'm afraid he's going to have to wait a while.'

'—right! I see. Yeah.' Weale said with awe, 'That's—that's terrific work—God, what a relief.' His voice took on an intimate tone, 'You know, I've been doing all the work here in the bar for the last twenty years, and—and all these years I've been sticking pins in Eddie's voodoo doll, and it turns out that—' It sounded as if he was coming close to tears, 'Poor bastard. Poor, poor bastard. All these years I've been thinking of him as just a leech and a— He was really a very good guy when I knew him, and—' Weale said sadly, 'I guess when you hate someone the way I thought I hated Eddie all these years, you kinda forget that— You kinda lose perspective and forget that he was once a real person and that he—that he—' He sounded lost for words. He said emotionally, 'Christ! I—I guess you know what I mean, huh?' He fell silent.

Feiffer said softly, 'Yes, I know what you mean.'

The Commander's voice said, risingly, 'Harry, the CIA. I've had the CIA on the phone, Harry...'

'Oh, yes, sir?'

'*Oh, yes, sir?* I'm glad you feel able to take it so calmly. Did you fully comprehend the three letters I used? *C-I-A?* Central Intelligence Agency—American Intelligence service? As in SIS, the *British* Intelligence Service who have *also* now rung me up asking why I'm having private conversations with the C-I-A . . . who the hell can I expect next, Harry? *The fucking KGB!*'

'One of my people got in touch with the American Embassy to check a detail of our current murder case, sir. He seems to have been routed to someone named Herxheimer in the CIA.'

'He didn't say his name was Herxheimer. He said he was' —he rustled some papers— 'Swingehaemmer.' He paused curiously for a moment, 'Well, whatever. I know the name of the local SIS man, who is no doubt at this very moment making a report to Whitehall, and his name, so far as I'm concerned, is *Thrown out on my Ear!*' He said threateningly, 'Explain, Harry.' He snapped before Feiffer could reply, 'And, Harry, a good beginning would be to tell me that the man you're after *isn't*—I repeat, isn't, *is not*—in Communist China!'

'He isn't in Communist China. To the best of our knowledge.'

'What do you mean, to the best of your knowledge? Is he or isn't he?'

'No, sir, he isn't.'

'Good. Where is he?'

'We believe he's either in Hong Kong or Macao.' Feiffer said consolingly, 'In any event, at the time, we weren't after anyone. At the time we were simply trying to establish the identity of the—'

'That blasted skeleton again!'

'Yes, sir.'

'And have you?'

'Yes, sir.'

'Then who is it?'

'It's an American named George Edward Putnam.'

'Definitely?'

'Definitely. He was killed over twenty years ago. Since then, someone else has been using his identity in order to defraud a bar owner here in Hong Kong through a branch of the Prosperity Bank in Macao.'

'I see.'

'Yes, sir.'

The Commander said, 'Oddly enough, when you explain it in that easy tone of voice that suggests you know all the answers, I'm inclined to think it's all fairly simple.' He asked, 'Is it fairly simple, Harry?'

'It is now, sir.'

The Commander sounded mollified. There was a silence from his end of the line. Feiffer could imagine him beginning to unbeetle his brow as he looked out his third floor office window at the ships and junks in the harbour, 'And all this spy stuff is just the cloak and dagger brigade earning their money? Is that right?'

'It's got no relevance to the case, sir.'

'Good. Good. I see. And this Communist Union fellow who keeps ringing me up about his cousin?'

'A thing of the past, sir.'

'Good. Good.'

'And, sir, I might add that I think our investigations, in a roundabout way, have improved police-Communist-secret society relations in the Portuguese colony of Macao—'

'Don't overdo it, Harry. You're pacifying me, but don't overdo it.'

'No, sir.'

The Commander asked, 'How long to close the case? Do you know who did it? This murder and fraud?'

'No, sir.'

'Who are your major suspects?'

'We don't have any.' Feiffer said quickly, 'To tell you the truth, sir . . .' (He thought he heard the Commander say something like 'Ha!') 'To tell you the truth, we've been expending most of our time and energy finding out who was done rather than whodunnit. Now we know that it's a matter of simply—'

The Commander said incredulously, 'Simply? Should I believe it? Or do you mean—'

'It's quite simple now, sir. All we have to do is put off a Coroner's Court for about six months and—'

The Commander said nothing.

'—and then have the victim of the fraud remit his usual payment to the bank in Macao and the Macao police can nail whoever turns up to collect it. Then it's simply (the Commander drew his breath again) a matter of standard (the Commander made a dubious snort) extradition back to Hong Kong and then—and then it's all over.'

The Commander waited. He asked cautiously, 'Is that all?'

'Yes, sir, that's all.'

'There's nothing else?'

'No, sir. Nothing.'

'Nothing can go wrong in this perfect little world of joy and happiness you're painting?'

'I don't see what.'

The Commander paused. He said slowly, word-by-word, in case one of the syllables might rebound back in his face and explode like a bomb with a trembler switch, 'Well—(nothing happened)—in that case—I congratulate you—(he gritted his teeth)—on a job well done.'

'Thank you, sir.'

'And you'll include all this in your daily report and I can show it to the various odds and sods who have been plaguing me—anything wrong with that idea?'

'Not a thing.'

'And that's right and simple and set and crystal clear, right?'

'Right, sir.'

There was a very long pause, then the Commander said, 'Harry, you've made an old man very happy. Very, very happy indeed . . . yes, a poor old man is—'

Feiffer said, 'You're not so old, Commander. Why, in my opinion—'

The Commander said in a snarl, 'Don't overdo it, Harry! I warn you, just don't overdo it . . .'

'No, sir.' Feiffer was still smiling as he put down the receiver.

Chagas' voice on the telephone said carefully, 'Harry, I'm sorry not to have rung earlier, but there were certain things we had to check. The statement from Pansy Yi and—' He said quickly, 'Everything she says still stands up so there's no need for you to worry on that score. It's just that—' He paused. 'Look, let me understand this: it's Putnam in the Morgue, isn't it?'

Feiffer said cheerfully, 'Yep.'

'That's what I thought.' He waited for a moment and drew a breath, 'Then—' he ran out of words, 'Um—listen, Harry, I don't know how to tell you this . . . but we've checked the fingerprints you sent us on the Army record against the ones the bank had on their payment slips. Now, before you say anything, we checked them on *all* the slips, not just the early ones, *all of them*, and then we went back and checked them again—that's why I'm late ringing you.' He said in a strained tone, 'And the impostor, the one with the phoney limp and the false beard . . .' he said, 'We've checked his fingerprints—all of them . . .'

Feiffer felt his entire body compress. He said in a strangled voice, 'And?'

Chagas said in a single breath, making the coup-de-grâce as quick and painless as possible, 'And the man who's been collecting the money all these years—there's absolutely no doubt about it—'

Feiffer said, '*What?*'

Chagas said, 'It's Putnam.'

Feiffer said, '*WHAT!!?*'

14

O'Yee had got his radiator working. In the bitter late winter afternoon the Detectives' Room baked in airless pulsing heat. The cat, its dreams of Caribbean ultra-violets transformed into reality, rolled over and stretched full-length on the floor. It arched its back, looked around with dull, hedonistic eyes, padded over to a spot midway between Spencer's and Auden's empty chairs, compared smells, and decided on Auden. It jumped noiselessly onto the chair and sighed, curled up, and, gazing briefly from one half-open eye at its mentor O'Yee, fell completely asleep. O'Yee said, 'I keep thinking that any moment Orson Wells is going to break in on the broadcast and tell us that it's all just a joke' —he saw Feiffer look quizzical— ' "The War of the Worlds": the radio broadcast where everyone thought the Martians were real and . . .' His voice trailed off, 'Well, you know.'

'It's no joke.'

'I didn't say it was. But he's The Man Who Never Was, isn't he? And you do realise that if what Chagas says about the fingerprints is true, then he's got a perfect right to do what he pleases. It's not against the law to put on a false beard when you go to pick up your own money, and it certainly isn't—'

Feiffer said sullenly, 'If it is Putnam who's picking it up.'

'Who else could it be? The fingerprints match—'

'We've only got Chagas' word for that.'

'You're not suggesting Augusto has some vested interest in—'

'Mistakes can be made.'

'Not with fingerprints. You're not trying to tell me that the Macao Police, who aren't exactly the Keystone Kops, can't even compare two sets of—'

'All right! So it's Putnam! All right? Are you happy now? It's Putnam! O.K?'

O'Yee said softly, 'O.K.' He settled his gaze on the cat, 'Is it too hot in here for you, Harry?'

'What the hell does that mean?' Feiffer shoved aside the Army and passport papers, 'Look, it's Putnam—O.K? All right? Satisfied? It's Putnam in Macao. It's been him all along, for the last twenty years, just trotting along happily and regularly to collect his dough—O.K? I admit it—all right? The skeleton isn't Putnam—it's someone else—all right? *Are you happy now?*'

'It doesn't make any difference to me one way or the other.'

'I know it doesn't make any difference to you! It never seemed to make any difference to *anyone*! I'm the only stupid bastard who's actually been treating the thing as if a real human being had been killed—to everyone else it's just some sort of running puzzle to go on the back page of the local newspaper along with the anagrams and the fucking cryptic crossword! O.K. so I was wrong—it isn't George Edward Putnam. George Edward Putnam is running around breathing and blinking and scratching his arse and wearing a false beard—all right?' He demanded, 'So who the hell *is* dead? You tell me, who the hell is it?'

'I don't know.'

'I know you don't bloody know!'

'Do you?'

'*No I don't!* And before you ask, I don't know why Putnam's teeth were found with whoever it was and I don't know why, if Putnam did him in, why he should make it look like himself when all the time he was charging about openly collecting his dividends! I don't know why he'd want to do that—I don't even know if that was what happened! And I sure as hell don't know who got killed! And I can't think of any way on Earth of finding out—*all right*?'

159

O'Yee nodded.

Feiffer said softly, 'For all I know, the set of dentures could have absolutely no connection with the skeleton at all. For all I know, Putnam could have simply dropped them there by total coincidence and somehow they could have—' He said, beaten, 'I don't know.' He took up the sheets of the passport and Army papers again, 'George Edward Putnam, ex-soldier clerk. Mister Average'—he pushed them away yet again, 'And there's nothing in here to tell me anything.'

O'Yee said reasonably, 'There's no motive, Harry. The only big thing in Putnam's life at the time seems to have been his partnership with Weale. If Putnam had just been found dead and Weale hadn't been paying him anything then obviously the number one suspect would have been Weale. But Weale has been paying him. For *years*.' He paused for a moment and scratched his head. 'But of course, it isn't Putnam who's dead, it's someone else. I just don't think there's any connection to it at all. What have you got to go on? Just the teeth and a vague feeling that—'

Feiffer said, 'And the limp.'

'Coincidence.'

'I don't believe that.'

'You have to believe it. Surely it's not beyond the realms of possibility that two men could have broken their ankles in Hong Kong sometime over the same two or three year period?'

Feiffer said, 'Not and have that teeth connection to link them.'

'But they're *not* linked! It really is Putnam in Macao!' He dropped his voice, 'Listen, I don't know why this case means so much to you, but you have to accept the fact that everything is against you in it. There just isn't any case.'

'And what about the passport? Why doesn't he use it? And where the hell does this breathing, walking-about, real, identifiable Putnam *live*?'

'I don't know. Does it matter? You're assuming everything in the world started from Day One when he was killed—whoever he was. For all anyone knows, Putnam could have perfectly good, albeit probably shady reasons for sneaking about undetected *that have absolutely nothing to do with the fact that there was a body found in Hop Pei Cove.*' He said in a concerned tone, 'You have to try and see the thing in perspective.'

Feiffer said nothing. His eyes strayed back to the papers. His attention seemed to fix on something, then almost instantly dismiss it.

'Do you see what I'm getting at, Harry?'

'Then why did Putnam plant his own false teeth on the body?'

'I don't know.'

'No, neither do I. And there's got to be some reason.' He nodded obstinately to himself, 'And if there's some reason, then there's some connection, and if there's some connection I intend to find out what it is.'

O'Yee said quietly, 'You really have a thing about this Putnam character, haven't you? All right. Get onto the Macao Police and ask them to pick him up in six months when he goes to collect the money. I don't know what it is you expect them to ask him: 'Pardon me, have you lost any teeth lately? Oh . . . say, twenty years ago? Yes, we did say, twenty. — Well, you see, there's this slightly obsessional cop in Hong Kong who thinks you killed somebody—well, actually, not actually *killed* somebody—to be honest, he thinks somebody killed *you*. And why do you wear a false beard? Because you like wearing a false beard? Oh. Well. Ah-ha—well, you may not know this, but that just happens to be a criminal offence here in Macao and we're very sorry but we're going to have to—" '

Feiffer said, 'Shut up.'

'And then what do they say to him? "Do you mind awfully if we extradite you to Hong Kong so the lunatic who put us up to all this can ask you some even sillier questions . . ."?'

'*There is some connection!*'

'Great! Then get witnesses! "Where were you on the night of . . . well, I don't know exactly which night . . . well, say, twenty years ago . . . well, say, at 9 p.m. at night—*well, I don't know, pick a night!*' '

'Goddammit, he's doing *something* illegal!'

'*What!*'

'Well—' Feiffer said, 'Well, I don't know!'

'All right then—*why*?'

Feiffer looked away. He said in the direction of the blazing radiator, 'No, Orson Wells doesn't come in on the airwaves and tell us that it was all just a joke. This War of the Worlds is real and there's a solution and I intend to find it.'

'There's a solution?' O'Yee said acidly, 'Wow! That's a relief. A solution. A solution to be had. A solution. Great!' He waited until he had Feiffer's attention, 'What is it?'

Feiffer said between gritted teeth, 'I-don't-know.'

'Does it occur to you that since it can all be explained away so reasonably and easily that maybe it *isn't* Putnam who's dead? And therefore, since he isn't dead there's no surprise in the fact that he's still alive. The teeth could be something quite accidental and totally unconnected (for all anyone knows, he could have simply dropped them there years later), and the only reason he's wearing a false beard is that—' He asked forcefully, 'Harry, does it occur to you that it's not a question of whether or not there's a solution, *it's a question of whether or not there's a bloody mystery in the first place*?'

'There is.'

'Which?'

'I don't know.' Feiffer looked away.

'You're getting as vague as—'

Feiffer said abruptly, 'I'll get him. I intend to get him.'

'*Who?* Get who?' He paused, 'And for what?'

He waited, and received no answer.

Dawson Baume's voice on the telephone said very softly, 'Harry?' He seemed to change his mind, 'Detective Chief Inspector, um, Feiffer?'

'Yes.'

'Um, this is'—he seemed to change his mind about that as

well— 'This is Doctor Baume at the Mortuary. I wondered if you had made any progress on the, um—'

Feiffer said, 'No.'

'I see.' There was a long pause in the sepulchral stillness of the dead room behind him, 'I've been thinking about the case and the—and the remains, and I thought that perhaps there might have been something you might have wanted in more detail, or, um—' Dawson had his unopened letter from Russia in his trouser pocket. He took it out and worried at the envelope with his free hand, 'Perhaps something that might not have been completely clear to you at the time or—' He got his fingernail under the stamp and flicked at the adhesive until he loosened it, 'Is there, um, anything like that—?'

'We seem to have come to a total blank wall on the case.'

'I see.' He moved the envelope into his palm and began squeezing it. 'I see.' He sounded very uncomfortable, 'But, um, the identification has gone all right, has it?'

'No.'

'Oh?' He cleared his throat. The envelope was crushed into a ball. He kneaded at it with his long, boney fingers, 'Um, in what way, if you don't mind my asking?'

'The person I thought it was turns out to be still alive. A man called Putnam.' He glanced across at O'Yee. O'Yee made a soft sighing noise.

'I see.' There was a pause. 'I see.' Dawson made a swallowing sound. 'I thought maybe that, um, if everything had gone all right and the information I gave you was of assistance, maybe by now it would have been all over and—' He said in an abrupt change of tone, 'The trouble with working alone the way I do, with all the resources of Science behind me is that— well, you tend to think after a while, if you're not careful—' He paused uncomfortably.

'Yes?'

'Well, you tend to think that you can never be wrong.'

'You weren't wrong. It's hardly your fault that it turned out to be the wrong man. You didn't identify him, I did.'

'From the false teeth.'

'That's right.'

Dawson Baume said, 'The ones that belonged with the body.'

'It's hardly your fault if—'

Dawson said suddenly firmly, 'Not the ones that belonged *to* the body.'

'What do you mean?'

'I mean that I just assumed that because they came with the skeleton that they were automatically—' He swallowed hard, 'I didn't try them in the mouth.'

'And have you now?'

'Yes.'

'And?'

Dawson said slowly, 'And they don't fit. Maybe I could have saved you a lot of time and effort. I could have used undertaker's wax to build up the gums under the contours of the plate and I could have—' In his hand the letter containing the Russian's vital move was crushed beyond salvage. 'I just didn't think to try them.' He said in the tone of a small boy, 'Harry, I'm very, very sorry. I—I just didn't think—'

'Forget it.'

'I'm really so sorry.'

Feiffer tried to put a good complexion on it. He said lightly, 'Well, what the hell? It was fun while it lasted and it looked like it had the makings of a pretty intricate puzzle. So it turns out to be just another unidentified body. God knows, there are enough of them around. We'll just let the money-collecting, false bearded, bloody limping Putnam hobble on in Macao collecting his loot and leave the case open for—'

'What do you mean?'

'I mean we've come to a dead end. To coin a phrase. (O'Yee looked at him and grimaced.) The real Putnam has a false beard and he—'

Dawson asked curiously, 'Does he still limp?'

'Still?' Feiffer said in a fatherly tone, 'No, the skeleton isn't Putnam. Putnam is alive. I don't know why he should have wanted anyone to think the skeleton was him—and to be honest I'm not even sure he ever knew anything about the skeleton—but—'

Dawson said, 'He wouldn't still limp. Not a chance. Not after all these years.'

'Who wouldn't?'

'Anyone with a break like the one I examined. Oh, he might have limped for a while, but he wouldn't still be limping after all these years. I may not know much about—' He said definitely, 'But he wouldn't still limp.'

Feiffer said confusedly, *'But it isn't him!'*

'Well in that case, perhaps it's just a coincidence and—'

Feiffer said slowly, 'A witness said the limp comes and goes.'

'Do you mean it's feigned?'

'It could be.' Feiffer asked, 'Why?'

There was a pause from the other end of the line, then Dawson offered, 'Maybe if he was trying to pretend he was the dead man he'd still limp because at the time of death the dead man limped. The killer, unless he was a medical man, would hardly know that a limp of that sort was only temporary. Maybe he thought it would be—' Dawson said abruptly, 'I really can't speculate. I'm really very, very sorry about—'

Feiffer said for the second time, 'Forget it.'

Dawson said after a moment, 'Does the real Putnam really limp or is it just a—'

'I don't know.'

'You've never seen him?'

'No.' Feiffer said slowly, 'Why should he? Why should he limp too?' He said softly into the phone, 'Who is he? The dead man.' He turned his gaze absently onto O'Yee. 'Who is he?'

At the other end of the line Dawson replaced the receiver gently. He looked down at the crumpled envelope in his hand. The antiseptic smell of the mortuary suddenly depressed him. He twisted his long fingers together. The smell of lysol and white tiles and death was suddenly very strong in the room. On the edge of tears, he began uncreasing the ruined letter.

Feiffer had his fist in a ball. He stared down at his desk and said yet again, '*Who is he?*'

O'Yee shook his head.

Auden made a grand entrance into the Detectives' Room trailing Spencer in his wake and vilified the gods: 'Well, that's it!' He fixed his Ancient Mariner's accusatory gaze on Feiffer, 'Well, you've done it for me! I'm done for now, finished!' He arrived at his chair, swiped the cat off in one almighty swipe of his still-scratched hand, shouted at it as it flew in mid-air, 'Fuck off!' and informed the world in ringing tones, 'I'm finished, humiliated, done for!' He waved his hands in an arc that dismissed the combined efforts of humanity to drag itself from the mud over the last six thousand years, 'I'm finished!'

O'Yee said softly, 'Well, that's a relief.' He looked with concern over to the cat. The cat had gone back to its bomb-proof building of files and folders. 'Do I take it you refer to the proceedings of The Crown versus Ong?'

Spencer went over and stroked the cat, at the same time looking at Auden sympathetically.

'I do refer to The Crown versus Ong, Senior Inspector O'Yee, yes.' (Feiffer was being ignored.) 'I refer to the fact that Detective Inspector Auden was made to look foolish by painting a picture of Ong as the local neighbourhood hood when all Ong is is the local neighbourhood intellectual criminal who I out-thought!' He gazed at Feiffer, 'I hope it was worth it! I hope you've got the whole skeleton case sewn up because I was the bloody sacrifice to it!' He refused to sit down. He began pacing up and down, declaiming. 'I had to make out that Ong was a vicious, dangerous criminal while all the while he sat there in the dock looking at the magistrates with a forlorn bloody look on his face! Do you know what he said to the Court? Do you? He said, "I'm a beaten man. I thought I was clever, but Detective Inspector Auden found me out with no trouble at all." *And then he asked my forgiveness.*'

O'Yee looked at Spencer interrogatively.

Auden shouted, 'Don't mind him! His reputation is riding high! He let his people have bail, all three of them! I had to oppose bail for one little mugger!' He fixed Feiffer with a terrible accusatory stare, 'Do you know what the North Point cops said to me? They said, "What's the matter, Phil? Afraid little Ong will come and get you in the middle of the night?"' He paused, took a deep breath and mimicked the North Point cops, not renowned for their tact, ' "Look at your mate, Bill Spencer, he's not worried about letting an armed gang loose—he's got 'em bamboozled. You ought to take bamboozling lessons, Phil—haw-haw-haw!"' He demanded from Feiffer, 'Well? The skeleton job—who did it? Where is he? I want to see the mad-dog killer I threw my reputation away for!'

Spencer said mildly in explanation, 'Phil had to say that he was afraid Ong might try to take physical retribution on him if he was granted bail.'

'How do you know?' Auden turned his ire onto the cat-stroker. 'How the hell do you know that? You were in the next Court letting out Machine Gun Kelly and his mates! How do you know that's what I said?'

Spencer said evenly, 'The North Point people told me.' He smiled lamely, 'The Prosecutor told them. It's, um, all over the—'

'DO YOU HEAR THAT?'

Feiffer said, 'I'd have to be deaf not to.'

Spencer shook his head warningly.

'Oh, you're all right if you're *deaf*! You can do what you like if you're deaf! You can cart bloody loaded pistols around and hold everyone up if you're *deaf*! It's only if you're a bloody five foot nothing skinny mugger that cops like Auden are terrified out of their boots about you! That bloody magistrate, at the end of the hearing, he said in his snotty little upper class voice, "Well I suppose if members of the police force fear for their lives then bail should not be granted." Then he looks straight at me, pushes his fucking glasses onto the end of his nose so he can have a really good down-the-hooter stare, sighs, and says, "Hmmm, perhaps police work may not be quite your natural line of work, Detective Inspector . . .?" ' Auden said, 'To me! I was the one who got Ong!' He stared at O'Yee, 'You're Chinese—(O'Yee started to say something) —you know all about losing face!'

O'Yee said evenly, 'It's not a thing a Chinese would discuss.'

'Ho-ho, you have a go at me too, why don't you? Everyone stand shoulder to shoulder to piss on Auden! How the hell is this going to look in my memoi—' He changed his mind and stopped suddenly.

Spencer said, interested, 'I didn't know you were writing your memoirs, Phil.'

O'Yee said, 'My Fifty Years in the Exotic East. Down the Trail of Villainy with Phillip Auden.'

'Ah, shut up!'

Feiffer said tonelessly, 'For your information, we got nowhere with the skeleton. So before you say it, I'll say it for you: your sacrifice was all for nothing.' He asked, 'Have you got any comments to make on that?'

'Yes, I have!'

Feiffer snarled at him, 'Then keep them for your fucking memoirs!' He jumped as Auden strode out and slammed the door behind him with a terrible detonation.

In the film version of *The War of the Worlds*, the flying saucers had come and vaporized everything with their hull-mounted ray guns. To Feiffer, at the moment, it seemed like an appealing thought. Auden had come back and had settled himself down to a late afternoon session of non-stop incoherent muttering and cursing, Spencer, still trying to pacify the flung cat, had got a saucer of milk from somewhere and was trying to coax the beast down from the shelves to sample it, and O'Yee was being disapproving.

Somewhere in the whole mess there had to be something. There had to be some tiny thing that . . .

He ran it over in his mind and came back to nothing.

Something. Some little thing left out or given the wrong

emphasis. The skeleton . . . Putnam . . . a man who limped . . . false beards—it all sounds like something from a Gothic . . . why would . . . anyone want to pretend that a skeleton was him and then go about openly and . . . and . . . why would . . .

None of it made sense.

He lit a cigarette. It tasted dry. It was almost five-thirty in the afternoon. He looked at the telephone and wondered whether it was possible to leave a message with the Commander's secretary. The Commander had no secretary. ("Excuse me, sir, but everything I told you earlier is rubbish. Putnam's still alive. I was wrong. Whoops . . . well, back to the old drawing board, aye, Commander? Commander? Sir?")
God almighty!

Auden said, 'You have to make a report to the Commander.' He grinned malevolently.

Spencer said, 'Gee.' He looked sorry for Feiffer. Feiffer thought that was the trouble with Spencer: he always looked sorry for someone. Feiffer said, 'I know that!' Auden kept the grin on his face. Feiffer asked O'Yee, 'What time is it?' O'Yee shrugged.

Auden said, 'It's time to ring the Commander, Chief Inspector, sir. Time for a little explanation about boo-booing.' He showed his teeth in a happy snarl. The cat went behind the folders and hid.

Feiffer said, 'Up yours, Auden!'

Auden, serene in revenge, widened the grin. He watched Feiffer's finger hover over the dial on the telephone.

The door opened and Weale came in carrying a briefcase. He looked expectant. He patted his over-ample barman's stomach and smiled.

Feiffer said, 'Mr Weale! Ah-ha!' His finger came at lightning speed away from the vicinity of the telephone. He said gleefully, 'Good to see you.'

Auden said miserably, 'Damn!'

15

Weale ran his hand slowly over the back of his bald pate in a gesture of resigned hopelessness. He had a burning cigarette in his other hand: he drew in smoke and expelled it in a long sigh. He sat down in a chair by Feiffer's desk, made a clucking noise with his tongue and then stared briefly at the floor.

Feiffer said quietly, 'I know I told you that he was dead, but, well, we were so sure ourselves, at the time.'

Weale nodded. 'There's no possibility of a mistake?'

'None. The fingerprints have definitely identified the man at the Macao bank as your partner.' He looked at Weale's face, 'It seems a bit odd having to break the bad news that someone's still alive, but I suppose in your case the news couldn't have been worse.' He looked at O'Yee. O'Yee said nothing.

'I've—' Weale looked up from the floor and put a brave face on it, 'I've been paying him for twenty years. It's, ah, it's nice to know that at least the money was going to him and not someone else.'

Spencer said softly, 'That's the best way to look at it.' He glanced around for the cat, but the thing was out of sight, still bunkered behind the files.

Auden asked, 'Any idea why he goes about in disguise?'

Weale asked, 'Who?'

Feiffer said, 'Putnam. He's been seen wearing a false beard when he goes to collect the money.'

Weale said, 'He is bearded—or at least he used to be. Are you sure it's a false one?'

'We're pretty certain.'

Weale said again, 'I don't know.' It was obvious he had lost interest in the details. He tapped his briefcase. For a moment he seemed on the verge of tears, 'I brought along all the stuff —the papers from my lawyer, the—all the stuff necessary to get him declared legally dead. All I wanted was an affidavit from the police and a copy of the death certificate and I would have been—' he paused for a moment. There was a catch in his voice, 'Free.'

Feiffer said again, 'I'm sorry.'

'Well, it's not your fault. You did your best and I don't suppose I should complain if you turned up the wrong card provided the game was honest.' He shrugged, 'So who was the dead man if it wasn't Putnam?'

'We don't know.'

'You've got no idea at all?'

Feiffer shook his head.

O'Yee said helpfully, 'For what it's worth, Harry's convinced that Putnam still has something to do with it—'

'What?'

Feiffer said, 'We're not sure about that either.'

'Do you mean Eddie might have killed this guy?'

'I don't know. I'd rather not go into that at the moment.'

'O.K.' Weale fell silent. He made a sniffing noise and wiped at his nose with a handkerchief, 'But I thought you said this guy resembled Eddie Putnam in every way—the skeleton? I mean, you said he limped and everything, just like Eddie—'

Auden said, 'Coincidence.'

'And that's it?'

Feiffer nodded. Weale seemed to have grown smaller as he sat in front of them, sinking lower and lower into the chair. His eyes had taken on a mournful beaten dullness. He brought the handkerchief up and sniffed, then wiped at his nose. He said very softly, 'Twenty years—more. More than twenty years Eddie Putnam's been eating away at me without a break and for the first time in all those years—' He shook his head, 'In all that time, I thought, just once, that I might have gotten free of him. That just once I could be my own man without that shadow hanging over me and bleeding me dry—' He said abruptly, the cheerful barman for an instant, 'Well, the few hours while I thought—well, it was good while it lasted.' He looked at Feiffer. 'I know you guys gave it your best shot and I really want to thank you for everything you did—really.'

Spencer said encouragingly, 'We might get him for something. For killing this other man, or—' He looked at Feiffer. Feiffer shook his head. 'Well, maybe something . . .' He smiled optimistically at Weale, 'I mean, you never know how things are going to turn out.'

Weale winked at him. 'Thanks, son.' He sniffed again. His eyes were glistening. He said softly to the room, 'Christ, it really can get you down when you spend all your life working for nothing. When you get a chance to be free and it turns out the thing that's been keeping you down all those years still has its claws firmly into your throat. He's a lot brighter than I am, is old Eddie Putnam, and you can bet your life that when you pick him up in Macao you'll find he's done nothing and he'll still be right at the same old stand short-changing me the way he always has—that's if you ever get him at all.'

'We'll get him the next time he goes to collect his money.'

'Eddie, Mr Feiffer? Don't you believe it. By now he'll probably have heard exactly what's happening and he'll still be one jump ahead of everyone else. I'll get a letter from Bombay or Timbuctu or somewhere out of your jurisdiction telling me he's changed banks and that'll be the end of it.' He said hopelessly, 'No, no one ever gets Eddie Putnam. You can't lay that bastard to rest. It's impossible.'

Feiffer said firmly, 'If he's guilty of anything we'll get him.'

'If?' Weale said, 'Yeah. If.' He shook his head, 'You know, sometimes I used to think that Eddie wasn't real, that he was just a conglomerate of—that he'd been dead for years just like your skeleton and that he'd no other purpose in the after-life except to drive me out of my brain. And, Jesus, so far he's doing a truly great job and someone up there or down there must be very happy with his work!' He said abruptly, 'Lousy bastard! The stinking, conniving lousy bastard! Jesus, when you people told me he was dead . . .' His voice dropped. He wiped at his nose again with his handkerchief. His voice was thickening as if he had a cold coming on, 'It's as if he's inside of me like a cancer and he's just rotting me away a bit at a time. And—and sometimes, when things are going all right and I think I've forgotten him for a while, he suddenly pops up again like this and I know he's still in there rotting me away like, like—' He sniffed heavily, 'Like I'll never be free of him!' He sniffed heavily, then sneezed. He put the handkerchief again to his nose and sneezed. He stood up to go, 'Well, anyway, thanks again Mr Feiffer.' He came forward and shook Feiffer's hand, then turned to take in O'Yee, Auden and Spencer, 'You all did your best and I'm grateful.' He paused and sneezed again, 'You're always welcome at *The Crap Game* if you're around that way.' He gathered up his briefcase from the floor and almost sneezed again. He said, his nasal passages blocked up, sniffing heavily, 'Must be something in here that I'm allergic to. Like, for example, the ghost of Eddie Putnam—'

Feiffer said quietly, 'I'm very sorry.'

'That's O.K. Why not? Well—' Weale waved his fist decisively in the air, 'Well, I guess it could have been worse. Maybe the bastard will turn up somewhere else dead. There must be a lot of people who'd like to see Eddie pushing up daisies and maybe if I wait long enough . . .' He concluded, 'Look, I'm sorry to have taken up all your time like this . . .'

Feiffer said, 'That's perfectly all right.'

'Yeah. Well, whatever, I think my sinus passages are telling me to get the hell out of here and feel sorry for myself back at home.' He sneezed again and demanded mock-angrily, 'Christ, what the hell have you guys got in here? A dead camel or something?'

Feiffer said, 'Just the corpses of extinct theories.'

'Yeah? I can believe it!' He said, 'Well, thanks anyway.' He grinned cheerfully at them all, 'Well, if ever you're in my part of town—you'll remember, huh?'

Feiffer nodded.

'Well—so long then.' He waved his hand and went out quickly.

They heard him sneeze once more in the corridor.

Feiffer asked in echo, 'What are we doing now? I'm glad you asked me that, Neal. What we're doing now is waiting for Orson Welles to come on the old steam radio and tell us all that it was all just a mistake brought to you by the Persil washing powder company of America and that none of it is really happening. That's about what we're doing now. We've just had in a less than happy citizen and he wanted to know what we were doing now too. Well, we told him and he left here virtually in tears, so I guess what we're doing while we're waiting for Welles is destroying lives. I'm getting pretty good at it. I thought I might apply for a transfer to Buchenwald where I can do it full-time.'

There was a long silence from the Commander's end of the telephone, then a slightly strangled voice said, 'You're going to tell me that . . .'

'Putnam's alive.'

'I knew it! I bloody knew it! I knew all this was too good to last! I bloody knew it!'

'Well, I'm fucking glad you did, because I bloodywell didn't up until—'

'What the hell's happened?'

'Putnam's alive.'

'You've already told me that. Where?'

'In Macao. There's no mistake. It's all been verified by fingerprints. He's alive. Or, to put it more succinctly, he isn't dead. The skeleton isn't him. So we're back at square minus one. We've got nothing.' He said in an excess of atonement, 'Do me a favour: demote me to Traffic.'

'Don't think I haven't considered it over the last few days! So what's the connection with the CIA and other assorted—'

'I don't know!'

'So what do I tell these people when they—'

'I don't know that either! Tell them Putnam was Chairman Mao's heir and the whole of the Peking Politburo is being turned over to him in the morning! How the hell do I know what to tell him?'

'You're getting over-excited about this.'

'Am I? Every way I turn this bastard Putnam has got it all over me! How the hell am I supposed to get: philosophical?'

'It might help.' The Commander asked, 'I hate to ask, but isn't Orson Welles that American actor with the odd voice?'

'Yeah, as opposed to that Hong Kong cop with the odd brain.'

'What has he got to do with all this?' His voice dropped several levels, 'I hate to ask . . .'

'He hasn't got anything to do with it.'

'Then why did you mention it?'

'Forget it. He did a radio play back in the thirties that—'

'Oh, yes, "The War of the Worlds." You're a bit too young to remember that, aren't you? Half of New York panicked and they had to stop the programme and tell people it was just a—' He said abruptly, the penny dropping, 'Oh, I see what you mean.' He went on in a slightly more sympathetic tone, 'Look, Harry, maybe all things considered, it might be best to pass this over to Special Branch. I mean, if this fellow's been moving about without a passport maybe we could palm it off onto them—'

Feiffer said, 'Yeah, maybe we could.'

'For some reason you appear to have got emotionally involved in this case. Maybe a new angle on it, someone fresh to it . . .'

'You're right. Give it to the CIA. Tell them Putnam's a Martian and maybe they'll pass it along to NASA and they can send up a rocket just like Orson Welles and—'

The Commander said cheerfully, 'So far I haven't been able to follow more than snatches of this case, but when it comes to things I can really be expert on I can tell you from the many grey hairs on my hoary head that in The War of the Worlds they didn't send up a rocket.'

Feiffer said wearily, 'Fascinating.'

The Commander went on chirpily, 'Nope, they were done in another way. I can even remember the line in the book—not all of us get our information from films and television, you know. Some of us—men of great learning—actually *read*.' (Feiffer looked at Spencer. The cat had surfaced and was padding warily towards Spencer's outstretched hand.) The Commander quoted, ' ". . . slain, after all Man's devices had failed, by the humblest things that God, in His Wisdom, has put upon this Earth." H. G. Wells. He used to be read the way people now read—' he failed to come up with a modern comparison, 'They were killed by microbes.'

'Were they?'

'Yes. The Martians. They were—'

The cat had reached Spencer's hand. It had curled itself against his wrist and was rubbing itself happily against his sleeve. Feiffer said, 'He sneezed.'

'Who did?' The Commander said evenly and carefully, 'Now, listen, Harry, maybe this case has—'

'*He sneezed!* He said there was something in here that—and the cat was—he couldn't see the cat because it was hiding behind the files and he couldn't—*but he sneezed*' He said suddenly, shouting, 'My God! It's him!' He yelled into the telephone, suddenly on his feet, 'God in Heaven, it's him!'

'*Who?*'

O'Yee and Auden had come over to the telephone. The cat had scattered from Spencer's hand and was fast disappearing back behind the files. O'Yee said, 'What? What?'

The Commander demanded, 'Who?'

Feiffer said, 'It's him!' His teeth were gritted. 'That's who it is—*it's him*!'

The Commander said, '*Who?*'

Feiffer said, 'PUTNAM!'

The Commander's voice said, 'Harry, I don't—' He heard a loud click as Feiffer, in the Detectives' Room, slammed down the telephone and, instantly, began dialling another number.

Phlebas the Phoenician, a fortnight dead,
Forgot the cry of gulls, and the deep sea swell
And the profit and loss.
A current under sea
Picked his bones in whispers. As he rose and fell
He passed the stages of his age and youth
Entering the whirlpool.
Gentile or Jew
O you who turn the wheel and look to windward,
Consider Phlebas, who was once handsome and as tall
as you . . .

Feiffer said slowly and carefully on the telephone, 'Mr Weale?'

In the background, the bar was open. 'Yes?'

'Detective Chief Inspector Feiffer. I'd like you to come in to the Station sometime this evening, if you could, please.'

The tone was ominous. Weale said after a moment, 'Why?'

'Oh, there are some questions I'd like to put to you.' Feiffer said with irony in his voice, 'If you're feeling composed enough after your emotional scene here earlier.'

There was another silence. 'Are you ordering me to—'

'Oh, I think you know at this stage that I'm not in a position to order you to do anything. What I'm asking you is whether or not you'd care to come to the Station of your own free will and have certain questions put to you, and undergo certain procedures.' He asked evenly, glancing at Auden at his desk, 'Are you willing to do that, Mr Weale? Or not?'

'Well, if there's any way I can help . . .'

'I'll discuss that with you when you come in.'

'And if I don't?'

'Why wouldn't you?'

It seemed, behind him, the bar had gone silent. Weale said in a tight voice, after a moment, 'You know, don't you?'

O'Yee was on the other telephone making arrangements for a search warrant. He shook his head to show that it was going to take time.

There was a long silence from Weale, then he said in a

different tone the same thing he had said at the Station earlier, 'He was eating me away, you know. Just like a—' He paused, 'Putnam. He's been eating away at me for—for over twenty years—' He must have put his face against the wall telephone. His voice sounded very close, 'God...'

'Will you come in or not?'

'You haven't—you haven't got the evidence, you know. Not for what you'd like.'

'Haven't I?'

'No, I've worked it all out and after all these years the evidence just isn't there. It's all circumstantial: the teeth and the—'

Feiffer asked, 'And the fingerprints?'

'They don't prove anything! Don't you see, they don't prove anything like murder at all! All they prove is—'

'They're a start.'

'That's all they are.' Weale said, 'And, and, the limp, when I told you about that I could have simply been mistaken—after all these years—that doesn't prove anything either and, ah—' Weale said, 'It was a corset, that was the limp. It was the girl in Macao who told you—I know you must have found her because—and the hair, did she tell you about the hair?'

'The beard.'

'Not the hair? That surprises me. She was so damned conceited that she once worked in some strip joint or other that she—she told you about the glue. I thought she smelled it on the hair.'

'The beard.'

'Amazing. Just that? Not half as clever as she thought, was she?'

'Perhaps not.' Feiffer glanced anxiously at O'Yee. O'Yee was saying, 'To search a premises in Woodcarvers' Road. Now. Immediately. Before the evidence can be destroyed . . . yes, *now* . . .'

Feiffer said to Weale, 'Is the story about winning a crap game true?'

'Yes.'

'And the partnership?'

'Yes.' Weale said, 'And the part about not wanting to work in the business. That night . . . at Hop Pei Cove . . . yeah.' He asked, 'You know everything about Putnam, don't you?'

'Just about.'

Weale said, 'He was eating me away . . . can you understand that? Eddie Putnam. Eddie Putnam, all these years, he's been eating me away.' He said in a whisper, 'You can't believe how much I've hated him all these years! Can you understand what that's been doing to me?'

'Come in to the Station and we can talk about it.'

'It wasn't an act—I really was disappointed that you knew you hadn't found him and—' He said again, 'I hated him. I really did hate him—all these years.'

'I know.'

'I know you do. I know you damnwell do!' There was another long silence as he must have looked behind him to the bar, his life's accomplishment. 'I don't know how you found out, but—' He stopped abruptly, 'You do know the truth, don't you? Christ, you do know, don't you?'

'Yes.'

'I always knew it'd come to this and I always thought—I thought when I was younger that I'd be able to stand it and get out of it because there was absolutely nothing to link me to him, but now, after all these years—' He almost shrieked into the phone, 'He's been like a disease! I've been like a man waiting around to die and I can't, and the disease just eats me away!' He begged, 'For Christ's sake, you do know, don't you?'

Feiffer said softly, 'The teeth seemed like the perfect idea at the time . . .'

'His fell out when he died. They went into the water and I—it seemed like—' He dropped his voice confessionally, 'The—the question arose of—of bashing his face in with a shovel—' He said so softly as to be almost inaudible, '—but I —I couldn't. I—I had a sudden premonition of what might— what the years might be like if he wasn't found for—and I couldn't do it. *I just didn't think he'd be found like this! So long after!'*

Feiffer pressed, 'And the disparity in build—Putnam medium and you—that was the reason for the limp, for the odd walk—a stomach corset. And Putnam always had a thick head of hair.'

'Yes. That was the wig and the beard and the corset, because—because—' He said desperately, 'Don't you see, that was the way Eddie Putnam looked twenty years ago! Not now! Twenty years ago! I've aged and I've put on a gut, but not Eddie Putnam. Eddie Putnam is twenty-nine years old forever. He never ages—like a ghost. *Eddie Putnam never grows any older!'*

Feiffer looked at O'Yee. O'Yee said into the telephone, 'Good. We'll be around in ten minutes to pick it up.' He nodded at Feiffer. Feiffer asked Weale, 'Will you come around?'

There was no reply.

Feiffer nodded urgently at O'Yee. O'Yee mouthed, 'Them too?' He indicated Auden and Spencer. Feiffer said with his hand on the mouthpiece of the telephone, 'Go! Go!'

Weale said very, very quietly, 'You know who was in that grave now, don't you?'

'Yes.'

There was silence from the bar.

Feiffer saw O'Yee and Auden and Spencer head out of the door. Feiffer said evenly into the telephone, 'It was you.'

'Yes.' Weale said, 'I suppose it was.' He said again, 'Yes.' He asked after a pause, 'What did it for you? I was the only one who could benefit both ways from Putnam being dead or alive, but that wasn't it, was it? I covered that. It was something small.'

Feiffer said, 'Putnam was allergic to animal fur. It was in his Army record.' There was a silence from the other end of the conversation, 'There was a cat in here. Not a dead camel. A cat. It was out of sight.'

'I see.' Weale said, 'I don't want to come in. You want

fingerprints, that's what you want.' He said airily, 'Well, I suppose I have to congratulate you on—but it's not much of a victory. All the punishment has been exacted already—twenty years' worth.' He babbled suddenly, 'I had to use all the disguises, the hair and the beard and the corset and—' He seemed to be sobbing, 'Because—'

Feiffer said gently, 'Come in now.'

'Because, God in sonofabitching Heaven, *I don't look like myself anymore!*'

'Yes.'

'I look like the man I killed! I look like the man I killed would have looked if he'd lived to be my age. I look in the mirror in the mornings and I see the man I killed! I just don't look like myself anymore! And in Macao I look like Eddie Putnam twenty years ago because—because Eddie Putnam never ages!'

Feiffer paused. He glanced at his watch. There was silence from the bar end of the telephone. 'Are you still there?' There was no reply. Feiffer said loudly, 'You! You!' He drew a breath, 'Putnam! Are you there?'

'Yes . . .' The pronounced Southern accent was there. It was the voice of a young man. Weale said softly, 'Yes, this is Eddie Putnam here.'

Feiffer nodded. He began to say—

'Poor old Charlie Weale is dead. I killed him near the beach one night twenty years ago. He didn't want to share the responsibilities, you see, and we argued and I killed him and stripped the body and used the teeth to turn him into—' He said in a small child's voice, 'Yes, this is Eddie Putnam here.'

'Come in and talk, Mr Putnam.'

Putnam said very quietly, 'I really didn't mean to do it, you know, but it's so long ago now and I—I just couldn't face having to be Eddie Putnam again after all these—and to hear that it was Charlie Weale that I—like being punished for your own suicide—' He said, his voice drifting, 'Even when I was at the bank and they all called me Mr Putnam it was like hearing someone's else's name and I—I changed back to Charlie Weale on the ferry and used my own—' He paused, '—Charlie Weale's passport to—I am Charlie Weale now—don't you see that?'

'Yes.' Feiffer urged him softly, 'Come in now.'

Putnam/Weale shouted in the crowded bar, '*I JUST DON'T KNOW WHO I AM ANYMORE!*' and, until O'Yee came on the line from the bar to say that they found the wig and beard and corset and the false papers hidden in the upstairs room of the bar and that the bar owner could not be located, Feiffer sat alone in the Detectives' Room holding a silent telephone with the cat rubbing itself archly around his ankles.

Even with the radiator still burning in the small room, there was the icy cold chill of long-death and extinction everywhere in the pores.

Hop Pei Cove

Bitter cold midwinter morning. A heavy mist coming in from the sea, clouding and bleaching. Something washing gently in and out on the ripples of tide-changing.

In the mist there was the sound of a buoy bell ringing hopelessly: a sea death-knell. Then there was no wind and the bell was silent, then a movement from the ocean and the bell went on ringing.

The body washed gently back and forth in the current, a drowning man still in his shirtsleeves, his fingers moving ceaselessly back and forth under the water placating someone, assuring someone that there was no cause for—that everything was settled and hopeful, fingers touching at the sand and making tiny transitory marks in the infinity of yellow grains . . .

Moving in towards the shore . . .

Sergeant Lew of the Water Police rang. He said efficiently and concisely, 'We've found a floater. Down at the same place as the skeleton. Bald, mid-fifties, European, it looks like he walked into the sea and killed himself. There are no signs of violence on the body.' He asked Feiffer, 'Do you want to handle it or shall we? It's in your area if you want it.'

'We'll take it.'

'Are you sure you want to?'

'We'll take it.'

'Any idea who it might be—for my report?'

'George Edward Putnam.'

Sergeant Lew said, 'Fine.' He paused a moment. 'Did you say *Putnam*?'

'That's right.'

Sergeant Lew said incredulously, '*Again?*'